Pursuit

By

Joan L. Anderson

2016

Pursuit © 2016 Joan L. Anderson
Triplicity Publishing, LLC

ISBN-13: 978-0996899499
ISBN-10: 0996899499

Printed in the United States of America
First Edition – 2016
Cover Design: Triplicity Publishing, LLC
Interior Design: Triplicity Publishing, LLC
Editor: Megan Brady - Triplicity Publishing, LLC

Dedication

To my wife, Barbara, for all of those times when you felt like a widow because I was off somewhere writing. Your love, patience and endless support helped to make this dream of mine become a reality.

And this book is also dedicated to the people of Paris, whose resolute strength and indomitable spirit have persevered despite the terrorist attacks in 2015. Vive la France!

CHAPTER ONE

"Ladies and gentlemen, this is your captain speaking. We've reached our cruising altitude of 35,000 feet, and it looks like we should have a smooth flight all the way into Paris this morning. The forecast for Paris looks good, with clear skies and a high of eighty-two degrees. So please sit back, relax, and enjoy the flight. On behalf of the flight deck and the cabin crew we'd like to thank you all for choosing Avion Airlines."

Claire pressed the button on her armrest and reclined her seat back as far as it would go, which was only an inch or two in the economy section. At least she'd managed to snag an aisle seat so she could stretch out her long legs, and the seat next to her was empty so she didn't have to elbow joust for the armrest. She leaned her head back and closed her eyes. The loud drone of the jet engines was nonstop and annoying, but at the same time it was sort of soothing, kind of like a white noise machine. One that weighed thirty-five tons. Finally, she thought, two weeks of peace and uninterrupted calm. No fighting with Kristine, and no worries about work. Nothing but lots of good food, wine, and decadent Parisian pastries. Just two weeks of taking care of herself and figuring out what the hell went wrong with her life.

She glanced at the woman sitting in the window seat. She was probably ten years younger than Claire, maybe in her mid-thirties. She was trim and looked like one of those people who did triathlons. The woman's thick, curly dark hair was cut in a cute short style, and she reminded Claire of a Caucasian version of Halle Berry. Her lightweight pink cashmere sweater molded her small, rounded breasts. The woman stared out the window, brows knitted, deep in her own thoughts, while she absently picked at the airline blanket over her lap. Good, Claire thought. Maybe I won't have to make idle chit chat for the next seven hours.

Closing her eyes again, she took a deep sigh. It was a good idea for her to go to Paris, she thought. After Kristine kicked her out of the house, *their* house, the house they'd lived in for seventeen years, for God's sake, the idea of just sitting in her stark new apartment on rented furniture, staring at the blank walls, would just push her deeper into her black funk. Christ, how could Kristine have dumped her? After all they'd been through together? After sticking to Kristine's side when she had breast cancer eight years ago, taking her to all of those doctor appointments, helping her through the surgery and chemo… Geez, that's gratitude for you. And Kristine complaining that Claire only thought of herself, never asking her anything about *her* work, or *her* family, or anything…she said it was always "Claire this", and "Claire that". She remembered Kristine telling her that she felt like she already lived alone, so she might as well just move out and make it official. In a way, she knew that Kristine was right. She had been consumed with work for a long time, but hey, she desperately wanted to be offered a partnership in her law firm, and that's the way the game was played.

Claire realized her jaw was clenched and her heart was pounding in her chest. Relax, she told herself, just take it easy. What's done is done, and nothing can change that now. I'll be damned if I'm going to let Kristine spoil a wonderful vacation, she thought. I need to move on with my life, meet new people, and have a good time. She reached down, rooted around in the oversized purse at her feet, and pulled out a set of headphones. She plugged the headphone jack into her armrest, scrolled through the music channels until she found some Mozart, and leaned her head back. Closing her eyes, she drew a deep breath, and slowly blew it all out. She folded her hands in her lap and tried to let her mind go blank, let all of the clutter and noise evaporate, and just focus on the music. A few rows behind her, a baby started to shriek and cry. Perfect. She cranked up the music.

"Would you like something to drink?"

The flight attendant stood at the beverage cart in the aisle, coffee carafe and tub of ice at the ready. She was the stereotypical flight attendant: young, pretty, and cheerful, her long blonde hair pulled back into a knot at the nape of her neck. Her red, white and blue scarf was tied at a jaunty angle at her throat, and her white blouse and navy blue slacks sculpted her perfect body like they had been designed just for her.

"Scotch, on the rocks, please." Claire brought her seat back up, unlatched her tray table and pulled it down.

The flight attendant scooped ice into a small, clear plastic glass, pulled out a little drawer with a clatter of bottles, took out a tiny bottle of scotch and handed them both to Claire. She plopped a small bag of pretzels on the tray table.

"How much is it?" Claire asked.

"They're complimentary on trans-Atlantic flights." The attendant looked at the woman sitting in the window seat. "Would you like anything?"

"Beer, please."

The attendant took a can of Heineken from the drawer, put a plastic glass upside down on top of the can, and handed it to the woman, then gave her a bag of pretzels. The flight attendant flashed a smile, and shoved the heavy cart three rows down the aisle.

The woman at the window popped open her beer and poured it into the glass, then took a long pull. She carefully wiped some froth from her lips and tore open the bag of pretzels. Lost in her own world, she went back to staring out the window, slowly munching on her pretzels, one at a time.

Claire poured the scotch over the ice and swirled her drink, watching the little ice cubes dance around the glass as they clinked into each other. She took a sip, and felt the smooth, smoky fluid warm her all the way to her belly. Much better, she thought.

She sipped at her scotch, letting her mind drift. She hoped the apartment she had rented in Paris was nice. It was in the Latin Quarter, which was one of the oldest parts of Paris. The apartment was close to the Sorbonne and the Jardin du Luxembourg, or Luxembourg Gardens. She imagined herself taking leisurely strolls through the gardens, down a warren of quaint Parisian cobblestone lanes, retracing the steps of Gertrude Stein and Hemingway. She'd stop at an outdoor café for a coffee, watch the people as they walked by, soak up the hot July sun, and just relax. She sighed. Maybe it would be fun. Maybe it would help her get over Kristine. God, she hoped she wouldn't be lonesome. The thought of being all alone in a huge city and not knowing another soul was terrifying. What if she got bored? Well, she figured she'd just have to wait and see what happened.

She finished her scotch, latched the tray table back in place, and tucked the empty bottle and plastic glass into the seat back pocket in front of her. She reached for the gray airline blanket wrapped in plastic at her feet, ripped it open, and spread the blanket over her lap, pulling it up to just below her chin. She put her headphones back on, reclined her seat all the way back, and closed her eyes, letting Mozart sooth her frayed nerves. Sleep. Sleep would be good. Make the time go by faster.

"Pasta or chicken?"

Claire opened her eyes. She must have dozed off. The flight attendant again stood at her side, the large metal food cart blocking the aisle, her attention focused on the woman in the window seat. Claire took off her headphones and unlatched her tray.

"Pasta," the woman said.

The flight attendant pulled out a small tray holding a roll, salad, and plastic coffee cup, then grabbed a gold foil-covered box, put it on the tray, and handed it to the woman. "Anything to drink?"

"Another beer would be great, thanks."

"What about you?" the attendant asked Claire as she handed the woman her beer, "Pasta or chicken?"

"Chicken, please." The attendant put a silver foil-covered box on another tray and placed it on Claire's tray table.

"Beverage?"

"White wine, please." The flight attendant took a small green bottle out of the drawer and handed it to Claire, then hauled the cart a few rows further down the aisle.

Claire peeled the foil cover off of her food. It looked like a meal designed for a toddler, with a single two inch stalk of broccoli, fragments of carrots the size of peas floating in a tan sauce covering shards of unidentifiable white meat, and a tiny brownie sealed in plastic wrap. The roll was as hard as a golf ball, and the salad consisted of half frozen lettuce, threads of carrot, and one tiny wedge of rock hard tomato. She poured the wine into her plastic glass, and took a sip. Oh, my God, she thought. Flying to France, and the airline serves crap like this. Oh well, she thought. It will be better once I get to Paris.

The woman in the window seat peeled the gold foil off her entrée to reveal the airline version of fettuccine alfredo, tiny flecks of parsley swimming in the white sauce. "Is this your first time going to Paris?" the woman in the window seat asked, smiling warmly. She twisted noodles around her fork, popped it into her mouth, and started to chew. Her earlier preoccupation with whatever it was seemed to have evaporated.

"Yeah, first time."

"This is my fourth or fifth trip. I love Paris." The woman smiled as she extended her hand. "I'm Suzie, by the way." There were little crinkles at the corners of her green eyes.

Claire took her hand. It was warm and soft. "Claire."

"Nice to meet you, Claire. So, what brings you to Paris?" Suzie took a sip of her beer, eyebrows raised expectantly.

Claire was silent for a moment, thinking about how she would respond. She focused her attention on ripping open the foil pouch of salad dressing. It was a struggle to tear the sturdy foil, and once she was finally able to breach it, a small stream of dressing shot out across her tray, dousing her lettuce, chicken, plastic ware, and tray table.

"Darn it!"

The woman chuckled. "That's happened to me so many times, I've lost count!" she said, shaking her head. "All of this stuff is probably packed at sea level, and then when it's opened up here at a lower air pressure, it just explodes. I've been "baptized" with yogurt, salad dressing, cream for my coffee…sometimes I wonder if I should wear a rain coat when I eat on a plane!"

Claire laughed as she pulled her pleated paper napkin out of its plastic sleeve and dabbed at the mess. Why *was* she going to Paris? That was a tough question to answer. She really didn't want to share all of the gory details of her love life and the break up with a total stranger. On the other hand, what did she have to lose? Maybe it would be good to vent with somebody safe, somebody who didn't know her from Adam, somebody she'd never see again. She wadded up her dirty napkin and set it on the tray.

"I just went through a messy break up, and thought it would be good to take some time and just relax."

Suzie looked genuinely concerned. "Oh, I'm sorry. That must be hard."

"Thanks. It was." She mixed the dressing with her lettuce, and took a bite. Not exactly haute cuisine.

"Had you and your boyfriend been together a long time?" Suzie asked as she took a forkful of her salad and slowly chewed.

"Girlfriend. Seventeen years."

"Oh. Well, a break up is a break up, I guess. I'm sure sorry." She paused for a moment and then asked, "Do you live in D.C.?"

"Just outside, in Virginia. How about you?" Claire took a bite of her entrée. It really wasn't too bad, despite how it looked. Could use some tarragon, though.

"Yeah, but I was born and bred in California."

"What do you do?"

"I work for the government, like almost everybody else in Washington."

"Which department?"

Suzie paused for an almost imperceptible moment, and then said, "Health and Human Services. I'm an administrative assistant." She buttered her roll and took a bite. An explosion of breadcrumbs cascaded to her lap. She brushed them off onto the floor. "You're going to love Paris. Do you speak any French?"

"I taught myself the basics…hello, good bye, thank you, do you speak English, where's the bathroom…" Claire smiled. "Should be interesting."

Suzie said, "A lot of the younger French speak English, even though they may not want to admit it. They take a lot of pride in their language and culture, and don't want to embarrass themselves by butchering English. But whatever you do, be polite, and be sure to greet everyone with *"bonjour"* and use a lot of *"s'il vous plaît"*. Suzie took another bite of her dinner, and said, "They're a very polite culture, even if most Americans aren't." She smiled again. "I remember the first time I went to the Louvre. I'd been there for hours and needed to use the bathroom, but I didn't know where one was. I saw a docent sitting on a little chair, and went over to her. She seemed like a real sweet, proper French woman. I said, *'Bon jour madame'*, and then in French I said I was sorry but I didn't speak much French, and asked if she spoke English. She said she did, so I asked her where the bathroom was. She told me with her cute little French accent that it was by the café, and to just "follow my nose" toward the smell of coffee. We both laughed, and off I went. A little while later I happened to walk by her again, and I saw this American woman go up to the docent and just blurt out, 'Where's the bathroom?' The docent looked at the woman, cocked her head and very politely said, *'Bon jour, madame,'* with a nod of her head. The American woman scowled and again said, with an attitude, 'Where's the bathroom?' and the French woman calmly repeated, *'Bon jour, madame.'* She never did tell the woman where the bathroom was. But boy, I learned my lesson…be polite, and the French will be wonderful and very helpful. But be a blunt, 'in your face' typical American, and you're on your own."

"Wow," said Claire. "I'll remember that."

"Flies and honey, baby, flies and honey."

Claire nodded and smiled. Suzie *was* kind of cute, in a perky sort of way. Then she mentally slapped herself. Jesus, Claire, what are you doing, she thought. Kristine just dumped you. Don't even go there.

After a while, the flight attendants came by and collected their dirty dishes and trash. Claire latched her tray back up and dug around in a side pocket of her purse on the floor. She pulled out the paperwork about her Paris apartment, and double-checked the address and the instructions as to how she would get the key. As she put the paperwork back in her purse, she glanced at Suzie and noticed that she was intently watching her.

"Are you staying in an apartment in Paris?" Suzie asked.

"Yeah. I'll be in Paris for two weeks, and it seemed like it would be more comfortable than a hotel."

"It really is. I've done that before, and it's nice not having to eat every meal in a restaurant, even if it is French food. This trip I'll be in a hotel, though. I'll only be in Paris for a day or two."

"For business?"

Suzie tipped her head to one side, thinking. "Yeah. Sort of. I guess you could say that."

Claire nodded. "Hmmm." She reached into her large purse again, pulled out a toothbrush and travel sized tube of toothpaste, then used her feet to shove the purse under the seat in front of her. She grinned. "Better get the broccoli out of my teeth." She unfastened her seat belt, struggled to hoist herself to her feet in the tight quarters, and walked down the aisle to the lavatory.

There were five or six people waiting in line for the toilets at the rear of the plane. The overhead lights had already been dimmed, and Claire gazed at the other passengers, still seated, in the semi-darkness. Some were wearing sleep masks and snuggled in their blankets, leaning against their friends or the side of the plane, sound asleep. How could they sleep in this cramped space with all the noise? Businessmen worked on their laptops, their faces illuminated by the glowing screens. Some people had their overhead lights on, reading books or doing crossword puzzles or Sudoku, while others wore headsets and watched movies on the small screens in front of them. Who were all these people, she wondered, and what were their stories? How odd that they should all find themselves here, together at this time, and once they landed in Paris they'd scatter like a flock of roosting birds after a loud noise, and never see each other again.

Finally, it was Claire's turn for the tiny bathroom. It was the size of a small phone booth, with barely enough room to turn around. How do large people manage? She stared at her face in the mirror. Jesus, she thought, you look like shit. Her brown eyes were like dull and lusterless buttons in her face, and there were dark circles under them. Her shoulder length, wavy brown hair was mussed and a little lopsided from having been against the headrest for hours. She was suddenly overwhelmed by loneliness and a deep sense of grief for having lost Kristine. She still loved Kristine more than she'd ever loved anyone, but there wasn't a damned thing she could do to get their lives back on track. Her eyes brimmed with tears. Stop that, she told herself as she wiped them away. Don't start.

She slowly shook her head in resignation. She brushed her teeth and spat into the micro sink, then pressed the little lever for the cold water to rinse the paste and spit from the sides of the basin. She ran more cold water and splashed some on her face, then pulled out some paper towels and dabbed herself dry. A sizable pool of water had accumulated in the sink. She depressed the shaft of the sink stopper, and with a slurp and a whoosh the water was quickly sucked down the drain. She ran her fingers through her hair, and went back to her seat.

She put the toothbrush and paste back in her bag, and looked at her watch. Still another three hours to go before they landed in Paris. She drew a deep breath and shifted in her seat, trying to get comfortable. She closed her eyes, leaned her head back, and fell into a fitful sleep.

The plane bumped once as it hit the runway, then rolled to the gate. As soon as it stopped people stood up, opened the overhead bins and pulled out their carry-on bags, jostling each other in the cramped aisle for space to set their suitcases down. Even those people in middle seats or next to the windows half stood, awkwardly crouching under the overhead bins, unable to stand up straight or go anywhere. Claire stayed put in her seat. She never could understand why people got up right away when it was always at least 5 minutes before the flight attendants opened the exit door and people began moving down the aisle.

Finally, the queue started to move toward the front of the plane. When there was a gap in the line, Claire stood and pulled her suitcase out of the overhead bin, slung her purse over her shoulder, and followed the other passengers down the aisle, with Suzie right behind her. Claire glanced at the rows of seats as she walked past. She was amazed at how much trash had accumulated in the seven and a half hour flight from D.C., and that it was all being left behind for somebody else to pick up. Crumpled blankets were strewn on the seats, plastic glasses and beer cans and coffee cups and newspapers were scattered on the floor and stuffed in the seat back pockets. Geez, people were pigs, she thought. She was glad she didn't have to help the cleaning crew deal with that mess.

Suzie followed Claire off the plane. As they entered the jet way, she pulled alongside Claire.

"Paris is a fabulous city," she said. "So much art, so much culture. I hope you have a great time. Maybe we'll run into each other, who knows?"

"Yeah, that would be nice." What were the odds in a city of two million people?

*

Terminal 1 of Charles de Gaulle airport is built like a giant octopus, with seven satellites reaching out from a central core. Nine arrival and departure gates are located in each of these satellites. Claire and the other passengers made their way from the gate to an underground moving walkway that carried them through a long, white tunnel toward Customs in the central core. The tunnel's rough textured walls reminded Claire of her mom's seven-minute icing, but she also thought that it looked suspiciously like asbestos. She tried not to think about what she might be sucking into her lungs. Claire pulled her suitcase along, alternately struggling to keep it close behind her when the walkway moved up an incline, then making sure it didn't get away from her or clip her heels as they went down a slope.

They finally reached Customs in the airport's main building. There were three Customs stations open, each with a uniformed, bored French official seated behind a bullet proof glass partition with a small slot beneath the glass just big enough for a passport to be slid through. Behind the stations were two French soldiers carrying automatic weapons, scanning the crowd. Two other very serious men dressed in suits stood near the soldiers. One was in his fifties, his thick gray hair combed straight back, icy blue eyes peering out from his weathered face, scrutinizing the line of people waiting to clear Customs. His broad shoulders and erect posture gave the impression that he had once been a military man. The other man was in his thirties with a thick moustache, broad shoulders and narrow hips. He looked like a guy who spent a lot of time at the gym. Both men were intently watching the crowd as it lined up for Customs. Claire noticed that they had tiny pins on their lapels, and then she realized that they were little American flags. Why would American officials be waiting at the French Customs counter?

There were seven or eight passengers in front of Suzie and Claire, and it took several minutes for them to slowly make their way to the head of the line. Finally, they were next, and when an elderly couple left one of the kiosks, the French official motioned for Suzie to come forward.

Suzie walked to the desk and smiled. "*Bon jour*," she said, and slid her passport under the glass partition. The Customs man opened it, studied it for a moment, then turned and looked at the two American men behind him. He nodded, and both men walked up to Suzie.

"Come with us, please, miss." The body builder took Suzie by the arm.

"Why? What's wrong?" Suzie said, looking from one man to the other. She jerked her arm, trying to wrest it free from his grip. "What's going on? Let me go!"

They led her away toward a door on one side of the station, Suzie struggling as they hustled her along. Suzie turned and looked at Claire, fear in her eyes, as they disappeared through the door.

CHAPTER TWO

Claire stepped up to the custom's counter and slid her passport under the little glass partition.

"Bon jour," she said, smiling. It always pays to be nice to the Customs guys, she thought.

"Bon jour." The bored French Customs man briefly glanced at Claire, and turned his attention to her passport on the desk. "How long will you be staying in France?" he asked.

"Two weeks."

"Where will you be going in France?"

"Just Paris."

"Where will you be staying?" The Customs man's fingers were poised over his computer keyboard.

Claire pulled the apartment paperwork out of her purse and read him the address, and he typed it into the computer.

"Please look at the red dot on the camera." Without looking up, the Customs man pointed to a small camera to the left of the counter. Claire glanced over, and heard a faint "click". The Customs man stamped her passport and slid it back to her. "Enjoy your visit."

*

The main building of Terminal 1 is a nine story, circular doughnut, with a sky-lighted central cavity. Multiple glass enclosed tubular moving sidewalks connect one level to another and crisscross this cavity. The whole thing seems very futuristic, and it looks like something straight out of the Jetsons.

Claire took one of the moving sidewalks to a lower level, walked down a short hallway, turned a corner and entered the unsecured, public part of the terminal. A crowd of people stood waiting for their friends and family who had just arrived. Several limousine drivers in black suits and chauffeur's caps stood holding signs with names on them, waiting to meet their parties: Deschamps, Perrigo, Hogan... An older Asian woman caught sight of a young Asian woman walking toward her carrying an infant, and as soon as she saw them she began to jump up and down, excitedly clapping her hands, squealing with delight. As the young woman and child reached her, the older woman scooped up the baby in her arms and spun around, gleefully and repeatedly patting the child on its back, planting kisses all over its face, and ignoring the young woman who just stood by passively and watched. Claire smiled...must be the first time Grandma has met her grandchild. She wondered if the daughter was offended to have been so badly ignored by her mother.

Claire stood, looking about to get her bearings, and spotted a cash machine near a coffee shop. Might as well get some Euros now, she thought. She used her debit card to withdraw two hundred Euros in cash and tucked the money into her pocket. She glanced around and saw a sign for "Shuttle" and "RER B to Paris" and followed it, dragging her suitcase behind. As she made her way through the crowd of other travelers and their luggage, she wondered what was going on with Suzie, and why she had been detained. She had seemed nice enough. Why would two American officials want to talk to her?

She got to the small shuttle station and waited on the platform with about 30 other travelers. All of them had suitcases of various sizes, some tiny and others gigantic, seemingly large enough to hold all of their worldly possessions. Everyone looked tired. After a few minutes the shuttle train arrived, and they all climbed aboard. There were only a few seats and most people had to stand, holding on to vertical metal poles or a plastic strap hanging from the ceiling. A few minutes later, they were at the airport's main train station.

Claire bought a ticket to Paris at the ticket office and went downstairs to the platform. Perhaps twenty other travelers were waiting, all with baggage in hand. After a few minutes a train arrived and the doors slid open. Claire lugged her suitcase on board, found a seat, and settled in. She saw the route map on the wall near the ceiling and noticed the stop for "St-Michel/Notre Dame", the station that she needed. She told herself to keep track of the stations along the way as they passed through them, so she wouldn't miss her stop.

*

It was a beautiful July afternoon. The train sped along, flanked on either side by tall vegetation that gave the impression of traveling through a green tunnel. Intermittently the train burst into a clearing, briefly exposing glimpses of ancient, pitted rust-colored stone houses that had survived god knows how many wars, surrounded by tall new apartment buildings and industrial parks.

Claire glanced at the others on the train. Quite an assortment of people, all of them with baggage in hand, seemingly from all over the globe. An elderly English couple, the man dressed in khaki pocket shorts and the woman in a pink floral blouse and slacks, studied their brochures and chatted about what they would do once they got to Paris. An African woman, her head wrapped in a bold batik scarf of blue, red and yellow that matched her long, flowing gown, had a wisp of a smile on her face as she attentively watched her toddler as he stood, swaying slightly with the rocking of the train, gazing intently into Claire's eyes. She smiled at him, and he shyly turned and buried his face in his mother's thigh.

Fatigue suddenly overwhelmed Claire, and she was dead tired. She had been up since 2:30 that morning, and it had been a long flight. She wanted nothing more than to just settle into the apartment and get a good night's sleep. She briefly closed her eyes, keeping a tight grip on her suitcase and purse, then thought better of it...what if she dozed off and missed her stop? She opened her eyes again, and struggled to stay awake and alert.

The train entered the outskirts of the city, and soon pulled into the station at *Gare du Nord*. Many of the travelers got off at this main train station in Paris, while throngs of other people climbed on board. The train was packed, and Claire pulled her suitcase closer to her legs in order to allow a well-dressed, older woman to sit on the seat next to her. The woman's hair was a solid chestnut brown, so uniform a color that it must have come from a bottle, and her eyebrows had been plucked into pencil thin half-moon arches, giving her a look of perpetual surprise. The woman gave no acknowledgment of Claire, but rather sat with a stone face and stared straight ahead. A young man in a crumpled shirt and tattered blue jeans edged his way through the crowd and stood in the aisle next to them, surrounded by a cloud of acrid body odor. The older woman next to Claire crinkled her nose in disgust and turned to look out the window, getting her nose as far away from the man as she could. The subway departed.

The train swayed slightly as it sped along while Claire monitored each stop that was passed. Soon it arrived at St-Michel/Notre Dame, and the doors opened. Claire stood and jostled through the people standing on the train, pushing against the sea of humanity trying to get onboard, and stepped onto the platform. She looked around and saw a sign for "*Sortie*" and began to walk in that direction. She passed a beggar sitting on the floor, her back against the wall. She was a woman of indeterminate age with large gaps where her front teeth should have been. She was wearing a headscarf and filthy long dress. One dirty hand was outstretched, her eyes pleading.

"S'*il vous plaît,*" she murmured. "S'*il vous plaît.*"

Both of her bare, swollen, blackened feet were twisted abnormally at a ninety-degree angle toward each other, her long, yellowed toenails curling under. Claire reached into her pocket, found some coins, and tossed them into the woman's cup. So different from the street beggars in D.C., Claire thought, most of whom looked like they were healthy and could easily get a job.

"*Merci, madame,*" the beggar muttered, her eyes pitifully gazing into Claire's.

Claire felt guilty, but grateful, as she walked away. Here she was, a "rich American" who had plenty to eat, clean clothes to wear, and a nice place to live, and had the money to go on a vacation half way around the world, while this woman struggled every day to even survive. She shook her head. She knew she was lucky to have the life that she did, and that there were millions of poor people in the world. Can't save them all, she told herself. But still…

*

She proceeded to the stairs leading to the street level and, using both hands, hauled her heavy suitcase up the steps. When she finally got to the top of the stairs, she set down her suitcase and stood for a moment, just looking around, drinking in Paris.

A steady stream of traffic flowed down the street in front of her, which ran parallel to the Seine River. People swarmed over the sidewalk, many of them with cameras strapped around their necks. Quite a few looked like they were retired Americans, wearing Bermuda shorts, white tennis shoes, and fanny packs strapped around their waists. A group of perhaps a dozen people passed by, gawking at their surroundings. A tour guide led the group, holding an upright, closed umbrella high above her head so the tourists could keep track of where she was and where they were heading. She was loudly rattling off something in German, pointing at various sights, the group turning their heads en masse to follow her pointed finger.

Vendors selling post cards and artwork had set up tables along the street. Some of the art looked like it was their own original paintings, but there were also small prints of Degas, Monet, and, of course, the Mona Lisa. Across the street was an open-air café where diners sat at small tables on the sidewalk. Waiters dressed in white shirts and black vests, white aprons tightly tied around their waists, wound their way between the tables. Low metal barricades jutted up along the edge of the sidewalk in front of her, a reminder for people to stay out of the street and traffic. She turned to her left and saw Notre Dame on an island in the middle of the Seine, its stained glass rose window spectacular even from this distance.

Claire dug into her purse and pulled out the email with the address of her apartment and her tourist map of Paris. Her apartment was near the Pantheon, close to the Sorbonne. She studied the map, and then looked around, searching for street signs. There were no signposts on the corners, or signs suspended above the streets. Crap, how does a person know where the heck they are? After a few moments of confusion, she finally noticed little blue placards with street names posted on the walls of the buildings at the intersections. She was on Quai Saint-Michel; looking at the map, she needed to go to the right to get to Boulevard Saint-Michel.

She walked two blocks down Quai Saint-Michel, wheeling her suitcase behind her through the crowds. She was obviously a tourist, and hoped that she wasn't a magnet for pickpockets the way a baby antelope attracts lions. She turned left onto the tree-lined Boulevard Saint-Michel and started up the hill, map in hand, suitcase at her heels. She made her way past a tour bus that was parked on the street with its engine idling. The middle-aged driver leaned against the bus and smoked a cigar as he waited for his passengers to return so the bus could move on to the next tourist spot.

After a few blocks she saw the sign for Rue Cujas on her left. She turned and strolled past the cafés and shops, searching for number 38.

Finally, she found it. The red painted door on an old four story stone building was tucked in between a café and a *tabac* shop selling cigars, cigarettes and newspapers. A lion's face was carved into the stone wall above the door and it scowled down at her, flanked by decorative stone rosettes. She glanced up at the building face and saw tall French doors leading onto tiny balconies on each of the floors, fronted by black wrought iron railings. A steeply sloped gray slate roof acting as both a wall and the roof capped the top floor, and dormers poked out from the slate. Window boxes brimming with vibrant red geraniums adorned many of the balconies.

Claire walked up to the door. To the left was an electronic digicode keypad. She re-read her email for the code, punched in "29896", then heard a faint "click". She pressed on the door, and it swung open.

The lobby was cool, with a well-worn, faded red Oriental carpet covering the cream-colored tile floor. The air had a faint musty smell, reminding Claire of her parent's basement in Seattle. A bank of locked brass mailboxes covered one wall, and on the opposite side was a Louis XIV straight chair and small table covered with a white lace tablecloth and a lonely crystal vase of artificial purple irises. A narrow staircase, bathed in deep shadows, was at the back of the lobby.

She dragged her suitcase to the darkened stairs. She spotted a light switch glowing orange on the wall by the stairs and pressed it. The lobby and stairs were suddenly bathed in light. It was a very tight spiral staircase, each pie-shaped step so narrow that if your foot was any larger than a small child's, you had to place it sideways on the step. Crablike, she climbed the three flights of stairs to the apartment, lugging her suitcase along as it bumped up each step behind her. Finally, she reached the apartment door.

There was a key under the doormat. She opened the door, and stepped in. The apartment was very small, but she had heard that was typical for Paris. Breathing hard from climbing the stairs, she put her bag and suitcase down, and looked around. A postage stamp living area had a small black vinyl couch and low coffee table, with a kitchenette across from it. French doors opened onto a tiny balcony, gauzy white curtains covering the windows. Claire took her suitcase into the bedroom and sat on the double bed, gazing around. A tiny nightstand held a porcelain lamp and clock radio, and a dresser sat against the opposite wall. Floral curtains covered the large window. A poster of the Eiffel Tower was above the bed. She was suddenly overcome with sadness, regret, and almost a feeling of mourning. What the hell am I doing here, she thought. Why couldn't I make it work with Kristine? Why didn't I try harder? She sighed, and shook her head with resignation. She got up and unpacked her clothes, hanging things up in the small closet and putting underwear and socks in the dresser.

She brought her toiletries into the bathroom, which was not much bigger than the restroom on the airplane. The walls were white, and blue tiles covered the floor. There was a tiny shower barely big enough to turn around in, with a hand held shower wand gingerly clinging to a standpipe. Matching blue bath and hand towels, as soft and absorbent as sand paper, were on the towel rack. She put her toothbrush, toothpaste and make-up on the small counter above the sink, and her hair products in the shower.

Claire went back out to the kitchen. The refrigerator contained a box of baking soda, but nothing else. She opened the cupboards and found a tin of coffee, a few tea bags, a package of spiral pasta, half a bottle of olive oil, and salt and pepper shakers. Better go out and get some groceries, she thought. She put her French dictionary in her purse, checked to make sure she had the key, grabbed her tourist map of Paris, and set off.

*

She walked back out to Boulevard Saint-Michel and glanced left and right. She could see the Jardin du Luxembourg stretching off to the left, so she turned right and re-traced her steps. About a block down the hill she noticed a shop across the street that looked like a French version of Albertson's. She went in, grabbed a shopping basket, and one by one walked down the aisles, exploring.

Claire picked up some cereal, fruit, and milk, and then sauntered past the cheese display. She was amazed at the variety of cheeses available, most of which she had never heard of. *Tome de montagne, laguiole, cantal, emmental de Savoie, chaource traditionnel*…she picked up a package and sniffed it. Hard to tell, but not too bad. She hoped it didn't taste like a stinky old shoe. She walked past the bakery section with its wide assortment of pastries, croissants, braided breads, and loaves of French bread. She put a crusty baguette in her basket, and then picked up a bottle of côte du Rhône on her way to the checkout counter.

An elderly French woman was checking out, chatting with the clerk in rapid French as her groceries were scanned. She was tiny, maybe five feet tall at best, with stooped shoulders and a large dowager's hump. Her white, curly hair was tucked under a pink beret. Despite the warm July weather, she wore a pink woolen jacket over her floral dress. Her pencil thin legs poked out from beneath her coat like a stick figure's, and they were covered with so many blue lines that they looked like a street map of Philadelphia.

The clerk was a young woman who quickly scanned each item and set it aside. She seemed to know the old woman, probably from years of being a customer, and warmly smiled as she spoke. As each item was scanned, the old woman put the groceries in her pull along cart. When she had finished, the woman paid for her groceries, and with a wave of her hand and a friendly "*au revoir*" she left, pulling her grocery-laden cart behind her.

Claire stepped up to the counter and smiled. "*Bon jour*," she said. The clerk didn't reply, but silently started to scan the groceries, then pushed each item onto the flat, open area beyond the scanner. Claire watched her work, and when she was finished, the clerk gave her a bored stare and said something in French that she couldn't understand. The woman who had been waiting in line behind her began taking groceries from her cart and putting them on the counter.

She met the eyes of the clerk, whose eyebrows rose expectantly, waiting. Claire looked at the cash register, saw that the total had come to 22.36 Euros, and handed the clerk twenty five euros. The clerk put the money in the till and gave her some coins in change, then started to scan the groceries of the next customer. All of Claire's items were still strewn across the end of the counter.

"Excuse me, but do you have a bag for the groceries?" Claire asked.

"*Désolé, je ne parle pas Anglais*", the clerk said, not looking up as she scanned the next customer's groceries.

"You have to bring your own bag when you get groceries," said the woman in line behind Claire. "Or you can buy one here." She was clearly an American, and sounded like she was straight from Boston. She looked like she was in her sixties and had short, gray, wavy hair, eyes the color of aquamarine, and pink scrubbed cheeks. She wore white Capri pants and a red sleeveless top. Like so many older American women, she was a little thick through the middle. As they were rung up, the woman put each of her items into her own shopping bag.

Claire stood motionless, not sure what to do. The American woman then said something in French to the clerk, who reached below the counter and brought up a cloth shopping bag. "*Deux Euro*," she said.

Claire smiled at the American woman as she gave the clerk a two Euros coin and started to bag her groceries. "Thanks for your help," she said. "I don't speak French, and this is my first time in France."

"Are you American, or Canadian?" the woman asked brightly as the clerk finished scanning her items.

"American. You sound like you're from Boston."

"Right-o." The woman grinned as she paid for her groceries. "But I've been living in Paris now for, oh, about eleven or twelve years. Judging by all the basics in your groceries, it looks like you just got here." The woman smiled as she hefted her grocery bag off the counter and started for the door.

Claire slung her own bag over her shoulder and walked alongside the woman as they left the store, then wound their way up Boulevard Saint-Michel. They passed a hair salon and a toy store, puzzles and dolls on display in the window.

"Just flew in this afternoon from D.C."

"Do you have friends in Paris?" the woman asked, shifting her shopping bag to her other hand as they walked along the sidewalk. "Careful," the woman said, pointing to a pile of dog poop on the sidewalk.

Claire stepped over the mess, and they continued to the corner. The light was red for them, but there was no traffic. The woman started to cross the street against the light. "Act like you're a Parisian," the woman said. "Everybody jaywalks."

They crossed the street, and continued down the sidewalk.

Claire moved her grocery bag to her other shoulder. "No, no friends. I'm here by myself. I just needed a little time on my own"

"Sounds like there's a story there," said the woman, smiling.

They passed an outdoor restaurant, a handful of people sitting at small round tables, couples chatting and picking at half empty plates of French fries and mussels. A Golden Retriever lay placidly at his owner's feet beneath one table, chin resting on his paws, and watched them pass by.

"I just got dumped after a seventeen year relationship."

"Ouch. Well, if you get lonely, a group of American ex-pats meet for dinner every Saturday night at a restaurant just down the road. Chez Henri, over on Rue Racine. You should come." The woman extended her hand. "I'm Sonja, and it's a real nice group of people." She laughed. "The same old gang has been doing this for years, so it's always nice to see a new face."

She shook her hand. "Claire. And I might just take you up on that."

They had reached a corner, and Sonja took a step toward the right onto Rue de Vaugirard. "I'm down this way. Any time after seven, and we'll be there. I hope you come, and if not, enjoy your stay!"

Sonja waved over her shoulder as she turned and headed down the street.

*

The afternoon sun was sinking low in the western sky, streaking the clouds with golds and pinks. It was still very pleasant and the sun felt good on Claire's face. As she walked a little farther down Boulevard Saint-Michel, her groceries began to cut into her shoulder. She shifted them to the other side and turned left on Rue Cujas and headed toward her apartment. She passed yet another small café, people sitting outdoors at wrought iron tables beneath red umbrellas. Waiters in black vests and long white aprons snaked their way through the tables. An older woman in a cream colored linen dress was sitting alone, sipping coffee, her West Highland White terrier asleep at her feet beneath the table. A young couple was chatting and laughing over their glasses of wine and a platter of hors d'oeuvres, the man's hand resting high up on the woman's thigh. A man in a silk suit was intently focused on his smart phone.

"Claire?"

Claire turned and looked at where the voice had come from. Suzie was sitting at a table near the café's door, waving.

"I can't believe I ran into you!" Suzie said, standing up as Claire approached. She gave Claire a big hug, bumping into the grocery bag over her shoulder. "Ooops, sorry!"

When she was released, Claire asked, "What happened to you in Customs? Is everything all right?"

28

"Oh, that," Suzie said, dismissively waving her hand in the air as she sat down again. "Just a misunderstanding. Apparently I look like somebody they were after. It all got straightened out. Are you staying nearby? Looks like you've been grocery shopping."

Claire shifted her bag of groceries to her other shoulder. "Yeah, I'm just down the street." She pointed in the general direction of the apartment. She was surprised at how happy she was to see Suzie. "Where are you staying?"

"Over by the Pantheon, in the Grande Hôtel Sorbonne, on Rue de l'Estrapade. Hey, do you want to get some dinner tonight?"

"Geez, I'm going to pass," Claire said. "I'm beat with the jet lag and all, and to be honest, all I want to do is get my groceries put away, have some wine and a quick bite, and call it a night."

"No problem, I understand," Suzie said. "It has been a long day. But hey, what about breakfast? We could just meet back here. They serve a wonderful *petit-déjeuner*."

Claire hesitated for a moment, but then said, "Sounds good. What time?"

"I'm sure we'll both be up early with the jet lag. How about seven thirty?"

"That sounds perfect."

Suzie dug through her purse and pulled out a scrap of paper and a pen, and began writing. "Here's my hotel address and room number, just in case."

Claire tucked the paper in her pocket. "OK. See you here at seven thirty."

*

29

She went back to her apartment and put the groceries away, then poured herself a glass of wine, sliced the baguette, put some cheese and grapes on a plate, and took it all out to the balcony. Sighing deeply, she sat at the little wrought iron table and sipped her wine, happy to finally be settled in the apartment. She glanced down at the street below.

Suzie had already left the café, and a waiter was clearing her dirty dishes and wiping off the table. A young man wearing colorful spandex bike shorts and a racing shirt pushed his bike along the sidewalk toward the Sorbonne. Claire noticed that he had one knee wrapped with a bandage. Must have taken a spill, she figured. She glanced at the building across the plaza from her. The building was four stories high, and a dozen small, short cylindrical chimneys bristled out of the top ridge of the building, looking like a lineup of coffee cans on the crest of the roof. The building had the same French windows and balconies as Claire's building. An older French man, his bare chest displaying a thick carpet of curly gray hair, leaned on his balcony railing and watched the young women go by on the sidewalk below. Across the street walked an older, gray haired woman, her ankles and feet so swollen that they looked like two footballs crammed into her sensible black shoes. She carried a shopping bag with a baguette poking out, her Yorkshire terrier proudly prancing along at her side.

Claire let her mind drift, and invariably it came around to Kristine. God, she wished Kristine was here with her. They could have had so much fun in Paris together. Exploring, eating and drinking good wine, making love… She sighed deeply. Never going to happen now. She suddenly realized that she was tired, tired to the core, and not just from the jet lag. She was tired with life. She shook her head with despair and got up, went into the apartment, and went to bed.

*

By 4:00 in the morning, she was wide awake. She got up and pulled back the bedroom drapes. A sprinkling of stars dotted the night sky. Looked like it was going to be another sunny, nice day. She brewed a pot of coffee and pulled out her laptop. Steaming mug in hand, she got online and checked her email. A few messages could wait, but she answered those from her office that needed a response ASAP. For crying out loud, they knew she was on vacation in Paris. Why were they still sending her urgent emails? But more importantly, she wondered, why was she answering them? Maybe Kristine was right, after all. She was a workaholic.

Claire finished answering her mail by 6:00 and turned off her laptop. She wasn't meeting Suzie for breakfast until 7:30, and she figured she had time to go for a quick run.

*

She changed into her jogging clothes and went downstairs to the street. Sunrise was just peaking over the buildings, its warmth turning the dew on the parked cars and ground into rising clouds of misty steam. The Latin Quarter was pretty quiet this time of the morning. The Sorbonne hadn't yet started classes for the day, and all of the students must have still been tucked into their little French beds. There wasn't much traffic, and only a few cars were parked on the street. Across from her apartment was an old, beat up sage green Peugeot, with a lone bearded man wearing a crocheted skull cap sitting in the driver's seat. Probably waiting to give someone a ride to work, she thought.

Claire started a slow jog down Rue Cujas and passed a *boulangerie* just opening for the day, the enticing assortment of pastries seducing passersby. She turned left on Boulevard Saint-Michel. A man wearing a fluorescent green vest swept the gutters with a broom that looked like it was straight from Amish country, its two foot long bristles snuggly tied around the broomstick.

She trotted through the wrought iron gate of the Jardin du Luxembourg then stopped, jogging in place for a moment, while she got her bearings. The Jardin du Luxembourg is the largest park in Paris, comprising over fifty acres of gardens. A broad, compacted dirt and fine gravel walkway, hard as cement, led to the center of the gardens, while another path went around the perimeter of the park. Claire wondered how many millions of feet, hooves, and carriage wheels had packed down this dirt over the last four hundred years. Wide expanses of grass were on either side of the path, with broad-leafed trees providing shade for the benches that were scattered throughout the park. Flowerbeds, bursting with color, dotted the grassy areas; vibrant purples, reds, lavenders, and white, surrounded by a low edging of repeating metal arches.

Turning to her left, she started to jog. She passed a vagrant curled up and asleep on a bench, his long stringy hair almost covering his face and gray stubbly beard, his clothes filthy and torn. A tattered backpack, probably containing all of his worldly belongings, lay on the ground next to him. Claire kept jogging, going past statues of long dead French kings and queens and gorgeous flowerbeds.

The air was filled with the sound of pigeons cooing, and she passed a flock of at least a dozen strutting around, pecking the ground for food, a quick head bob with every step. She ran past empty tennis courts, and a grassy patch where a handful of people were doing their slow, graceful dance of tai chi. It was soothing, even just watching them.

She finished jogging the loop of the gardens and was soon back at the gate on Boulevard Saint-Michel. She stopped, hands on her knees, catching her breath for a moment, panting out puffs of steam into the cool morning air, then slowly walked back home. Once there, she quickly showered, threw on her clothes and make up, grabbed her purse, and went to meet Suzie for breakfast.

*

Claire was at the restaurant right on the dot of 7:30, but she didn't see Suzie. She ordered a *café crème* and sipped her coffee, watching the people go by on their way to work or school. She waited. No Suzie. She ordered a second cup of coffee and waited longer. Still no Suzie. When Suzie hadn't shown up by 8:00, Claire wondered if she had forgotten, or had overslept. She dug in her bag and pulled out Suzie's address. Room 314, the Grande Hôtel Sorbonne. Maybe she'd walk over to her hotel and see what was going on. She put some Euros on top of her bill in the little saucer on the table and left.

*

The Grande Hôtel Sorbonne was a four-star hotel with gilded mirrors in the lobby and brocade draperies over the large windows, with gold braided, tasseled tie backs holding the drapes open. The smartly dressed desk clerk smiled and said "*Bon jour*" as Claire entered and made her way to the elevator. She pulled open the outside elevator door then stepped into the tiny space. It wasn't much bigger than a phone booth, its walls painted light blue, with a mirror on the back wall to give the impression that it was larger than it really was. Claire noticed a sign above the floor selection panel that said "4 *personnes*, 300 kg". She smiled, and shook her head. Four people, huh? In this tiny space? Only if they were kids or super models, she thought. She pressed the button for three, and the inside doors slid shut. The elevator rumbled, then stopped. The inside doors slid open, but the outside door remained closed. Claire noticed a brass panel on the door that said "*poussée*" and she pushed on it. The door swung open, and Claire stepped into the darkened hallway. She saw an illuminated orange button on the wall and pressed it, lighting up ornate gold chandeliers running down the corridor. The room right across from the elevator was 308.

The hallway was painted deep navy blue, with cherry wainscoting and moldings and thick, gold colored carpeting. Claire glanced again at Suzie's hotel information, and then slowly walked down the corridor, searching for room 314. She could hear the faint sound of a vacuum cleaner coming from a room down the hall behind her. Finally, she found 314, and tapped on the door.

"Suzie?" She waited a minute, but there was no response.

Claire tried the doorknob, and was surprised when the door opened. Inside, the hotel room was dark.

"Suzie, you awake?" She groped on the wall for the light switch, and turned on the light. She gasped.

Suzie lay on her back on the bed, her wrists bound together and tied to the headboard. There was a gaping, deep red wound where her throat has been slashed, and a dark burgundy pool had oozed onto the pillow on either side of her neck.

CHAPTER THREE

Claire gingerly stepped over to the bed. Suzie's dead, cloudy, lusterless green eyes stared blankly at the ceiling. Her dark hair was matted with the blood that had saturated the pillow. A cloth gag had been crammed into her gaping mouth. Her shirt had been ripped open, and half a dozen small, round, red wounds were on her chest.

"Oh, shit. Oh, shit." Claire felt a little lightheaded. Don't faint now, she told herself. She looked around the room. It had clearly been tossed. Suzie's suitcase lay open and empty on the floor, and clothes were strewn everywhere. Whoever did this must have been looking for something. Drugs? Money?

I've got to get out of here, she thought, panic welling up inside her chest. What if the maid comes by and finds me here? I'd be screwed. She ran her fingers through her hair. All right, she thought, let's just think about this. Take it easy. Do I call the police? No, they might think I was involved. She knew nothing about the French legal system, and remembered that American student, Amanda Knox, and how the Italian courts had sentenced her to twenty-six years in prison for the murder of her roommate, even though there was no evidence that she had been involved in the crime. Would the French courts do the same thing to her? Hell, she thought, I just met the woman yesterday! I really don't know anything about her.

She furrowed her brow, put her hand over her mouth, and tried to concentrate, willing herself to be calm, to breathe slowly. Suzie's dead, and there's nothing I can do about that. Have I touched anything in the room? Left any fingerprints or DNA? No. What about the door? She remembered that she had touched the doorknob when she came into the room.

Claire went back out into the hallway. She could still hear vacuuming down the hall. She wiped the doorknob with the bottom of her shirt and paused…could they get her DNA from her shirt? It had been against her skin, after all, and it may have picked up some skin cells. Better not take the chance. She went back into the hotel room and quickly walked to the bathroom, trying not to look at Suzie's body as she went by. She tore off a few squares of toilet paper and went back into the hallway. She wiped the doorknob with the toilet paper, stuffed it into her pocket, and quickly walked toward the elevator. The vacuuming had stopped. How long would it be before the cleaning staff found Suzie? Claire glanced down the hall and froze. There was a security camera on the ceiling, pointing right at her. Too late…its bright red blinking eye showed it was active, and it must have already spotted her. There was nothing she could do about that now. She continued to the elevator and took it downstairs.

*

Traffic was just starting to build on the street, and people streamed along the sidewalk on their way to work. Claire wasn't sure what to do. She slowly walked back toward her apartment, desperately trying to sort out all of the thoughts swirling around in her head. She was still a few blocks from the apartment when she spied a *boulangerie* with a wide assortment of pastries on display in the window. Her stomach growled at the sight of the food. I need time to think this through, she thought, and I haven't eaten anything since the wine and cheese last night.

She felt guilty treating herself with pastries while Suzie lay dead just a few blocks away, but she told herself that she still had to eat, and having something in her stomach would raise her blood sugar and help her think more clearly. She went in and bought a raspberry filled pastry and a cup of coffee, then walked to the Jardin du Luxembourg. She found an empty park bench beneath a linden tree and sat down. She set her coffee on the bench, slipped half of the pastry out of its little paper sack, and took a bite. Oh, my god. It was so flaky and wonderful, the raspberry sweet yet tangy, little flakes of pastry clinging to her chin and falling on her lap. It would have been heavenly, if she hadn't just stumbled upon a dead body. She took a sip of coffee, and stared into space. Geez, what a day. What was she going to do? What if the police were able to track her down by the hotel's security camera footage, and thought she was involved? Would they believe her if she said she had nothing to do with Suzie's death? And what the hell happened to Suzie, anyway? Was it a robbery gone bad? Something else? Was it linked to Suzie's problems at Customs? This sure as hell hasn't turned out to be the relaxing vacation she was hoping for.

She sipped her coffee and ate her pastry. Should she go to the embassy? No, probably better to just keep her head down and not say anything. The more she thought about it, the more her logical, analytical, attorney's brain took over. Well, she thought finally, there's nothing I can do about it now, and it really isn't my problem. She nodded to herself decisively. It was really too bad, and she was very sorry Suzie was dead, but she needed to just let it go and move on. But how? She thought about what would be a good, mindless, soothing distraction for the rest of the day, and decided she'd go to the Notre Dame cathedral on the Seine. Maybe she could find some peace and comfort in "God's house."

A Middle Eastern man with a full beard, wearing a long white linen robe and small red skullcap walked down the path and stopped at a bench across from her. He sat down, pulled out his cell phone, made a quick call, and slipped the phone back into his pocket. He casually glanced around the park, and then seemed to focus his attention on Claire.

She took the last bite of her pastry and crumpled the bag. She finished off her coffee, then strolled over to a garbage can and tossed her trash into the bin. She started to head for the park exit on Boulevard Saint-Michel, but before she got very far she could feel someone watching her. She turned and glanced behind her, and saw that the man on the bench had also gotten up and was following about a hundred feet behind her.

Claire turned left on Boulevard Saint-Michel and started walking down the hill. She noticed a "tacky tourist shop" with a rack of post cards of the Eiffel tower, Notre Dame, and the Seine partially blocking the sidewalk. She stepped into the shop and looked around. One entire wall displayed T-shirts with "*J'aime Paris*" or bold sequined Eiffel Towers plastered across their fronts. She walked around the store, passing counters stacked high with shot glasses and coffee mugs with "Paris" and "I heart Paris" on them, commemorative plates with pictures of the arc de triomphe, key chains of little blue, red, and gold Eiffel towers, and mounds of berets in every color. Should she get Kristine a souvenir? Probably not.

She walked out of the shop and glanced back up the street toward the Jardin du Luxembourg. The bearded man seemed to be window-shopping two stores down, his cell phone pressed to his ear. He glanced toward Claire, and went back to staring at the shop window. Claire turned and walked north down the hill toward the Seine, winding her way through the crowds. After a block she cast a quick peek over her shoulder. The bearded man was still there, walking thirty feet behind her. Claire felt a little knot of panic in her belly. OK, she thought to herself, just stop it. You're being silly. I'm sure there's nothing to worry about. And there are a lot of people around. Nothing's going to happen.

She turned right onto Boulevard Saint-Germain, then left on Rue Saint-Jacques. She turned to look, and the man was still following her. The small knot in her stomach tightened. Claire broke into a jog, turned right onto the quai de Montebello that ran along the Seine, and darted into a café.

"*S'il vous plaît, où est votre WC*?" she asked the man at the bar, thankful she had learned how to ask where the bathroom was in French. He pointed toward the rear of the restaurant and said, "*Voilà.*"

Claire went into the rest room and closed the door behind her, leaning her back against the door, breathing hard. Shit, that can't be a coincidence. Can it? She closed her eyes, willing herself to be calm. Why would he be following me? What if he's out there waiting for me when I come out? What do I do? She stepped to the sink and splashed cool water on her face, then dried off with a paper towel. She looked at herself in the mirror. She had dark circles under her eyes, and tension lined her face. What have you gotten yourself into, she wondered. I never should have come to Paris. I should have just stayed home and worked it out with Kristine. Too late now.

After a few minutes, there was a knock at the door. "*Madame? S'il vous plaît, j'ai besoin de la toilette.*" Apparently the woman at the door "had to go", and as a result, so did Claire.

When she stepped out of the café, she looked up and down the street. No sign of the bearded man in white. Whatever that was all about, it was over now. She took a deep sigh of relief, and blew it out slowly. She could see Notre Dame looming ahead. Since I'm this close, she thought, I may as well go see it.

The Seine was a murky sage green and sluggish, with tour boats tied up along its bank. Flights of cement stairs led from the street level down to broad walkways along the river's edge. Claire walked over the Place du Petit Pont that crossed the Seine. There was a short line of tourists waiting to enter the cathedral. While she waited in line, she glanced up at the church. It really was a magnificent Gothic masterpiece. Unlike so many other cathedrals, the main focus was not an ornate, pointed steeple reaching heavenward. Instead, the two front corners were square towers, and between them was a central round rose window of stained glass, looking like a giant kaleidoscope frozen in time. Gargoyles scowled over the square below. Claire pulled out her tourist book and thumbed through until she found the section on Notre Dame. Geez, it was old!

She read that Pope Alexander III laid the first stones in 1163, and it took 170 years to complete the cathedral. She looked again at the church, and imagined the hundreds of men who had been involved with its construction, and the sweat and blood that they had literally poured into it in

41

an era before power tools and heavy machinery. Claire wondered what they would have thought if they could have known that 850 years later, people were still admiring their craftsmanship.

The line inched forward, and finally Claire stepped into the cool interior of the church. The stained glass rose window above the altar truly was spectacular, casting blue and red prismed light onto the nave. She strolled around the church, admiring the statues of long dead popes and French emperors. She stepped across stone crypt markers set into the tiled floor covering the graves of dead priests from the 1700s. She marveled at the Pietà behind the high altar and the statues of the Virgin Mary and Child scattered throughout the church. There were half a dozen dark oak, ornately carved wooden confessionals along the sidewall. She wondered how many secrets and sins had been confessed in them over the centuries. Had Napoleon asked for forgiveness for having had his mistresses? For leading thousands of French men to their deaths during his Napoleonic wars?

She ambled to the central nave of the church and sat in a pew. She closed her eyes, folded her hands in her lap and just soaked up the peace and serenity enveloping her. She could so easily stay here all day, and not think at all about Kristine or Suzie or the bearded man… She savored the quiet for several blissful minutes, then sighed deeply and stood up. Better get back to reality.

She walked to the exit and stepped into the bright sunshine. She glanced around the plaza in front of the church, and froze. The bearded man was leaning against a low cement barricade in the square, arms folded, looking right at her. He stood up, and started walking toward her.

Claire broke into a run, elbowing her way through the crowd waiting to enter the cathedral, and turned right onto Rue du Cloître Notre Dame that goes along the north side of the church. Gargoyles glared down at her as she sped past. She glanced over her shoulder and saw the man quickly following her. She ran faster.

She dashed over the Seine on the Pont de l'Archevêché, fighting her way through the crowds. The bridge's railings were solid walls of gold padlocks. Even in her panic, Claire remembered hearing about this bridge, and how lovers would attach locks to the railings, signifying their never ending love for each other. Her relationship with Kristine flashed into her mind. They always thought their love would last, too, but it didn't. How many of these lovers were still together?

She was breathing hard, gasping for air, her lungs burning, but she knew she couldn't slow down. Once over the Seine, Claire turned left onto the Quai de la Tournelle, and shot a quick glance behind her. The man was running forty feet back, his white robe billowing out like a sail behind him, and he was quickly closing the gap.

She saw a city bus just ahead, starting to close its doors. She ran toward the bus, frantically waving her arms. The bus driver saw her and opened the doors. Claire jumped on board, walked down the aisle and took a window seat, her chest heaving as she tried to catch her breath, sweat dripping down her face and neck. The bus pulled away and entered traffic as the bearded man stopped and stood on the sidewalk, breathing hard, hands on his knees, and watched it go.

*

Claire got off the bus a few blocks from her apartment and walked home, her thoughts swirling like a dust devil inside her head. Why would that guy be chasing her? Were Suzie and the bearded man somehow connected? Do I go to the police? And say what? That my friend was murdered and yes, I was there and found her, but I had nothing to do with it and the boogey man has been following me? She knew it all sounded crazy, and she really didn't want to get wrapped up in Suzie's death.

It was almost three o'clock when Claire got back to her apartment. When she unlocked the door, she froze. Couch cushions had been flipped up, every cupboard in the kitchen had been opened and emptied, their contents scattered across the countertops. She walked through to the bedroom. The dresser drawers had been dumped on the bed, her clothes looking like a load of laundry waiting to be folded. Claire sat down on the bed and looked around at the chaos surrounding her. What the hell was going on? She felt like she was in the middle of a terrible nightmare, but couldn't wake up. She sighed and shook her head. Well, better clean this mess up.

As she worked, she tried to come up with a logical explanation for what had been happening. It had to all be connected. But how? What the hell was going on? She wished she could talk to somebody. Should she call Kristine? No way, she thought, I can't do that. I'm an intelligent, capable, grown up woman. I need to think this through, figure this out for myself, and not go running to Kristine at the first sign of trouble.

It took her awhile, but finally the chaos in the apartment was all sorted out and order was restored. She poured herself a glass of wine, got some cheese and fruit and went out to the veranda. She sat there, munching slowly, sipping her wine, and letting her thoughts drift like a leaf in a stream. She glanced at the apartment across the street and noticed the older man once again out on his balcony.

He wore a short-sleeved plaid shirt, open at the throat and halfway down his chest. Their eyes met. He smiled and nodded once in acknowledgment. She raised her hand in reply, and then looked away. No need to encourage the old guy.

She spent a long time on her balcony, musing, trying to sort everything out, but no rational explanation came. She was suddenly overcome with bone-dragging fatigue. A combination of frustration, stress, jet lag, and the wine, she thought. It had been a hell of a day, and she had nowhere she had to be, and nothing she had to do. She looked at her watch. Seven fifteen. Not even dark yet, but close enough to bedtime. She put her dirty dishes in the sink, went into the bedroom, stripped down, and crawled into bed. Sleep quickly engulfed her like a tsunami.

*

Why doesn't that damned woodpecker stop tapping? And why is there a woodpecker in my room?

She slowly came up out of her dream and realized someone was knocking on the door to the apartment. Morning light was streaming in through the window. She pulled on her robe and slippers and padded her way to the living room.

"Who is it?" she asked.

"*La police. Ouvrir la porte, s'il vous plaît.*"

"I'm sorry, I don't speak French," Claire said through the closed door.

"Open the door, please," a man's voice said. "I am with the police."

Claire could feel her chest tighten with apprehension. She double checked the security chain on the door and opened it a crack. A middle-aged man wearing a rumpled gray suit held up his police identification and badge. Claire's fingers fumbled as they unlatched the chain, then she opened the door and stepped back.

"Are you Claire McKenna?" the man asked as he stepped into the apartment and closed the door behind him. He slid his identification back into the breast pocket of his suit coat. His mouse gray hair was thin on top, and his doughy face had deep wrinkles across his forehead giving him a perpetually pensive look. He reminded Claire of a basset hound, brown doleful eyes that looked like they had seen all the misery that the world could offer, and ears with long earlobes. The smell of stale cigarette smoke clung to him like the cloud of dust that surrounds Pigpen in the Peanuts comics.

Claire pulled her robe more tightly around herself and crossed her arms. "Yes."

"I am Inspector Girard. I would like you to come down to the police station with me, if you please. We have some questions for you."

"About what?" Claire asked, although she thought she probably already knew.

"We will talk at the station. Please, if you would get dressed. And I would like your passport, please."

*

The *Commissariat de Police* was just south of Notre Dame on rue de la Montagne Sainte-Geneviève. Claire sat on a straight-backed metal chair in an interrogation room. The room was stark, with gray walls and cement floor. Easier to clean up body fluids and vomit, she thought. A square commercial clock was on one wall, and a built-in mirror consumed the upper half of the wall across from Claire. She assumed it was a one-way mirror, and she wondered how many people were on the other side, silently watching.

Inspector Girard sat across from her, casually leaning back in his chair, hands folded in his lap, her passport on the steel table in front of him. A second officer, a younger man with a Roman nose and close cropped hair the color of nutmeg, flipped through a file, intermittently casting glances up at Claire.

"An American woman named Suzie Nichols was murdered the other night at the Grande Hôtel Sorbonne. Did you know her?" Inspector Girard cocked his head to one side, waiting for an answer.

Claire rested her folded hands on the table. "I sat next to her on the flight from D.C. to Paris. I wouldn't say that I really knew her." Claire's mind was racing…how much to say? How much do they already know? How did they even track her down in order to interview her? She noticed that her knee was nervously bouncing up and down. Stop it, she told herself, and put one hand on her thigh as a reminder to keep it still.

Inspector Girard shot a quick glance at her leg, then returned his attention to her face. "You were seen leaving her hotel room the morning she was killed. Would you like to tell us about that?" Inspector Girard's eyes bored into hers. Claire felt he was searching deeply into her soul, searching for truth, searching for lies.

Claire shrugged. "Like I said, I met her on the plane, and ran into her in Paris. We were going to have breakfast together. When she didn't show up, I went to her hotel to see if she had overslept. She was already dead when I got there. It was horrible." Claire thought for a moment before asking, "Do I need an attorney?"

Inspector Girard leaned forward, placing his palms flat on the table, his eyes intent on Claire's face. "Why, have you done something wrong?" The other policeman kept jotting down notes, occasionally glancing up at Claire, then more notes.

"Of course not. But I don't know anything about how the French legal system works."

Inspector Girard smiled with wry amusement. He looked at her passport on the table, and placed one finger lightly on one corner, slowly spinning it around in small circles, thinking. After a few moments, he folded his hands, and looked up at Claire, still smiling. "You think perhaps I am like Inspector Clouseau in "The Pink Panther" movies?" His smile quickly faded, and his face became deadly serious. "I assure you, we are nothing like that." His intense, searching stare returned. "We are only interested in the truth, *madame*. But it is up to you if you want an attorney."

Claire thought about it for a minute and shook her head. "No, I haven't done anything wrong." She folded her hands on the table and leaned forward, matching his posture, and met his gaze. "How can I help you?" Her knee started to bounce again.

Inspector Girard briefly glanced at Claire's knee, and she immediately nailed her foot to the floor.

Inspector Girard stood up and slowly walked around the table, passing behind Claire. "After you discovered Madame Nichols, why did you not call the police?"

She resisted the urge to turn and look at him, but rather kept staring at the mirror across from her, focused on his reflection. "I told you, I don't know anything about the French legal system. I was afraid I'd be incriminated." She made a conscious effort to breathe slowly.

Inspector Girard came back to his chair and sat down, a perplexed look on his face. "Incriminated?" he said to the other officer. "*Qu'est-ce que c'est?*"

"*Impliquer,*" the other officer said.

Inspector Girard nodded, smiling briefly. "Ah, yes," he said. Then the smile quickly disappeared. "Yet, here we are."

The room was silent for a few moments, Inspector Girard intently watching Claire's face. Claire was familiar with this tactic from her own interviews with clients. Silence can become so uncomfortable; it will often make a person start to talk just to break the oppressive stillness. The only sounds in the room were the faint ticking of the clock on the wall and the low hum of the air conditioner. Finally, she said, "I'm curious. How did you find me?"

"Your photo was taken when you went through Customs at the airport. And you gave the address where you would be staying in Paris."

She nodded thoughtfully. "I don't know if they are related to Suzie, but odd things have been happening to me."

Inspector Girard raised his eyebrows expectantly. "Such as?"

Claire took a deep breath, and slowly blew it out. May as well tell him everything. "After I found Suzie dead,

I went to the Jardin du Luxembourg to think about what had happened. I was there for maybe fifteen minutes, and when I left, a man followed me all the way down to Notre Dame. He ended up chasing me, but I was able to get away."

"What did he look like?"

"He looked Middle Eastern. Bearded, in a long white robe. And then when I got home, my apartment had been broken into. It looked like it had been searched."

Inspector Girard scowled, confused. "Why would anyone follow you or search your apartment?"

"I have no idea."

No one spoke for several minutes. Finally Inspector Girard gave Claire an appraising look, and then muttered something in French to his colleague. He slid the passport to the other officer, who slipped it into the file and closed it.

Inspector Girard stood up. "That is all that we will need, for now, Madame McKenna. Thank you for your help. We will keep your passport, for the time being. Please, do not leave Paris. We may need to talk with you again. And if you have any more difficulties, please let us know."

CHAPTER FOUR

As soon as the phone started to ring, she knew it had been a mistake to call. Too late.

"Hello?"

Claire paused for a moment, gathering her courage, swallowing hard. "Hi, Kristine, it's me." She leaned back on the couch in her living room and nervously ran her fingers through her hair. A half-eaten sandwich and some grapes waited on a plate on the coffee table in front of her. She picked some invisible lint off her pant leg.

The line was so silent, Claire wondered if they had been disconnected. "What do you want?" Kristine finally said, a hint of hostility in her voice. Claire could hear a stifled yawn.

"I had to talk to somebody, and I didn't know who else I could call." Her knee started to nervously bounce again. She put her hand on her thigh and held it down.

The edge to Kristine's voice was as sharp as a guillotine. "It's six o'clock in the fucking morning. You woke me up. What's so important that you had to call?"

Claire put her hand over her eyes, and started to softly cry.

"Claire?" Kristine's voice had softened, suddenly filled with concern. The old Kristine. "What's the matter, honey? Are you ok?"

"I don't know," she sobbed pitifully. She unburdened herself and told Kristine everything, about meeting Suzie, finding her dead, the man following her, the break in, the police.

When she finished, Kristine gently said, "Jesus, Claire. Do you think you want to just come home?"

"I can't," she sniffed, wiping her nose on the back of her hand. "The police took my passport."

"What are you going to do?"

She ran her fingers through her hair again with frustration. "I don't know," she whimpered.

Kristine was quiet for a few seconds, and then said with finality, "Well, just think about it. What's done is done. I mean, really, what else can go wrong?"

Claire sniffed up some snot. "No, shit. Can't get much worse."

Kristine continued, "I mean, it's too bad Suzie was murdered, but you had nothing to do with that. Who knows what she was into that ended up getting her killed. And if you have any more problems with being followed, the police will look into it." She paused for a moment before going on. "You're in Paris. You've always wanted to go to Paris. I say, just put it all behind you and enjoy yourself. Go to the Louvre, see the Eiffel Tower, go to Sacré-Coeur. Go to all of the places and do all of the things you've always wanted to see and do."

"I know," she said, sniffing. "You're probably right. But it's hard to get the image of Suzie lying there dead, her throat slit, out of my head."

Kristine's tone softened. "Well, that's understandable. But try, will you? I mean, really…there's nothing you can do about any of this, and none of it has been your fault.

What's done is done." She paused to give it a chance to sink in. "Right?"

Claire was silent for a few moments. "I suppose. I just feel so bad about Suzie, and I hardly even knew her."

"I know. You're only human. But try, will you? Try to get past it, see some of the sights, and have a good time while you're in Paris."

She nodded, her logical attorney's brain finally kicking in. "You're right. Until the police give me back my passport, I don't really have a choice. I'm stuck here, so I have two options: stay in the apartment and mope, or get out and try to enjoy Paris." She paused for a moment and nodded, having made up her mind. "Thanks, Kristine. I really needed that."

"Not a problem."

"And I'm sorry to have woken you up"

"Don't worry about it. We've been through a lot together, and even though we aren't a couple anymore, I still want us to be friends. And this is what friends do." She paused for a moment and added bitterly, "Even at six o'clock on a Saturday morning."

"You're the best. Thanks."

"Keep me posted, ok? And you'd better bring me a great souvenir, after all of this!"

Claire hung up. She felt a whole lot better; but then, she always did after talking to Kristine. And Kristine was right, she thought. Nothing she could do about any of this, so she might as well try to enjoy Paris.

*

She decided to get some air, and walked back to the Jardin du Luxembourg, hoping she wouldn't see the bearded man again. She strolled through the park and spotted a stand selling coffee, hot chocolate, ice cream and soft drinks. She bought a cup of coffee, sipping it as she casually ambled through the park. Older women walked their little un-neutered dogs straining at their leashes, testicles boldly bouncing between their legs. Apparently the French don't believe in doggie birth control, she thought. Young couples sat on blankets spread on the grass, embracing, lightly kissing each other. A middle aged man led four ponies down the path with a delighted, bike-helmeted child proudly perched on each one, swaying with the rhythm of every step of the pony. Claire grinned. Too cute. Little French cowpokes.

The sun felt good on her shoulders as she walked down the paths, past grassy lawns and flowerbeds. She stopped at a large pond surrounded by families with small children, the children brandishing long, rubber tipped canes that they used to launch toy sailboats, two feet long, across the pond. The boats all sported flags of different nations: Spain, Great Britain, Norway, Russia, Italy. The children would squeal with delight when their boat careened into another, bump off, then head in a new direction. Claire smiled. Such simple pleasures, and such a delight to see families out enjoying the gorgeous July day. And for her not to think about Suzie or the bearded man.

After watching the kids for a while, she glanced at her watch. Almost 6:30. She realized that tonight was the night the ex-pats met for dinner. It might be a relief to spend some time with other Americans. No police, no accents, no struggling with a language she didn't know, no cultural norms to worry about; just relax, meet some nice people, and have some good wine and dinner.

She arrived at Chez Henri a little after seven. The restaurant was open to the sidewalk, and the outside tables were packed with diners. Inside, the restaurant was elegant but cozy with warm apricot walls, white linen tablecloths, and small vases of flowers on the tables. The padded chairs were covered in matching apricot slipcovers. Claire scanned the room and saw Sonja and three other older people at a table in the back corner.

Claire wound her way through the restaurant, the low murmur of conversations and clinking of cutlery surrounding her. Sonja saw her as she approached, and waved. When she got to the table, Sonja stood and gave her a big hug.

"Claire, I'm so glad you came! I didn't think you would. People, this is Claire, and she just flew in from the States a few days ago." Claire pulled out a chair and sat down. A young waiter with a long white apron tied snugly around his waist appeared at her side.

"Something to drink, *madame*?" he asked.

"A glass of côte du Rhône, please," Claire said.

"Very good," he said, and left.

"Let's not be formal," Sonja said. "Introduce yourselves, folks."

The woman seated across from Claire extended her hand. "I'm Helen, and this is my husband, Peter." Helen had warm brown eyes the color of Hershey's syrup, and thinning spiked brown hair with blond highlights. Peter's gray, close-cropped hair was receding, and his short white beard vainly tried to hide his double chin. Twinkling, intelligent gray eyes peered out from behind his gold wire-rimmed glasses. His short-sleeved plaid shirt was snug across his plump belly, with little gaps showing between the buttons. Claire couldn't help but think he looked like Santa Claus on summer vacation.

"Welcome," said Peter, smiling.

The other woman at the table looked Middle Eastern. She wore a beautiful light blue, satin gown with embroidery on the bodice, and she had a matching scarf that was set back a little on her forehead and draped over her shoulders. Streaks of gray were scattered throughout her jet-black hair. Claire thought she was strikingly beautiful. "I'm Roshni," she said, flashing white teeth.

"It's good to meet all of you."

"Likewise," said Peter with a nod.

The waiter returned with Claire's wine, then left.

Claire briefly swirled her wine glass, and took a sip. Oh, god, that was good.

"So what made you all decide to move to Paris?" she asked.

Helen smiled and said, "Well, Peter had been with the State Department in D.C. for years and there was an opening at the Embassy here. We thought, what the heck? Why not? Our kids were all grown up and gone, and it was just the two of us. Paris seemed like a fun place to spend a few years." She turned to Peter. "And that was, what, nine or ten years ago?"

"Closer to fourteen," said Peter.

"No! It can't be that long! Where does the time go?" She shook her head slowly in disbelief.

"What about you, Roshni?" asked Claire.

Roshni pursed her lips, leaned back in her chair, and took a deep sigh. "It's complicated," she said, folding her hands on the table. "I was born in Iran in 1946 when the Shah was in power. Iranian political history is complex and full of intrigue, but suffice it to say that the Shah was a brutal despot who ruled with an iron fist. Nevertheless, I was able to go to school, got married, had a baby, and got a good job. But the political situation in Iran just got worse and worse. It was so bad that in 1970 Amnesty International declared that Iran had the worst human rights record of any nation on earth. It finally got to be intolerable for us, and in 1978 my husband and I decided to leave Iran. We emigrated to France, and spent a few years in Nice before our visas came through to go to the United States. We became naturalized U.S. citizens in 1986."

"That must have been hard," Claire said.

Roshni nodded. "It was. Being uprooted like that, leaving our families behind. But we survived, and actually thrived in the U.S. My husband worked as an engineer for Boeing, and we had a good life. 'The American Dream.' Nice house, nice cars, our son got an MBA from Columbia …but all of that changed with 9-11. Suddenly, just because we were Muslims, we were the enemy. Our mosque was bombed, and people, even strangers on the street, treated us with contempt. We just couldn't believe it was happening. We'd always been good Americans, and proud to be American. But the bigots couldn't see that. We put up with it for a few years, but when we started to get death threats, we said 'enough'. My son had a great job and a girlfriend in New York and wanted to stay in the States, but my husband and I moved back to France in 2008. Things were better here at first, because there are a lot of Muslim immigrants in Paris. But lately, there's been resentment against the Muslims here, too." She shook her head. "I don't know when it will all end. Something needs to be done, but I don't know what." She was quiet for a moment. "Then to make it even worse, my husband died of pancreatic cancer last year."

"I'm so sorry," said Claire with heartfelt sympathy.

Everyone was quiet for a moment. Finally, Roshni shook her head, and gave a wry smile. "Well, that certainly put a damper on the party!"

"That's all right," Sonja said, patting Roshni on the hand. "It's just unbelievable how some people can be so stupid and prejudiced against a whole culture, and paint all of the people with the same broad, hateful brush. There are some bad apples in any group, whether it's Muslims, Christians, Jews, minorities, Caucasians… But the more you learn about different groups of people, the more you see that most people are basically good, and the bad ones are an exception.

They all nodded in agreement.

Claire turned to Sonja. "What about you, Sonja? Why did you move to Paris?"

"It's kind of a long story. My uncle was killed at Dunkirk in the Second World War, and once Paris was liberated my aunt had to find some way to support herself. She opened a *patisserie*, and had it until she died about twelve years ago. I was her only family, so she left it to me. I was an only child and never had any children and didn't have any other family in the States, so I thought "Why not? I'll move to Paris." I've always loved to bake (I guess it runs in the family!) but there are a million *patisserie*s and *boulangerie*s in Paris. So I thought, rather than keep it as a French bakery I'd do something different, and decided to sell American baked goods. The bakery's called American Pie, and so far, at least, it's been successful."

"What do you make?"

58

"Things they usually don't have in Europe, like pies. The Europeans have tarts, but pie is a strictly American dessert. So we make apple, cherry, lemon meringue, coconut cream, chocolate cream, and pecan pies, as well as cinnamon rolls, chocolate chip cookies, snickerdoodles... We even do Rice Krispy treats. It's surprising how many Parisians come in for our baked goods."

"That's fabulous," replied Claire with a grin.

"So, Claire," Helen asked, changing the subject. "How do you like Paris? Are you having fun?"

Claire knitted her eyebrows, and sadly shook her head. "I have to say, this is the worst vacation I've ever had."

"Really?" Roshni said incredulously. "Why?"

Claire took a deep breath and filled them in on everything that had been happening to her. When she finally stopped talking, they all just sat silently, staring at Claire in disbelief. At last, Roshni said, "Geez. That's awful. Maybe you should go back home while you still can."

"I can't," Claire said bitterly. "The police took my passport."

"Well," said Roshni, "on behalf of all the Muslims in Paris, I apologize for the problems that one man has caused you."

Claire nodded in appreciation. "Thanks, but like Sonja said, you certainly can't blame a whole culture for one bad apple."

Helen turned to Peter. "Can the State Department do anything to help?"

He raised his eyebrows and shrugged. "I'd be happy to talk to the police for you and see if there's anything the Embassy can do," he said, "but to be honest, it probably wouldn't make any difference. It's their legal system, after all, not ours."

Claire thought for a moment and sipped her wine, then shook her head. "Thanks, but that's ok. I'll just let this play out and see what happens. I'm sure it will be fine."

Peter took out his wallet and handed Claire a business card. "If you need anything, just let me know."

"Thanks." She tucked the card in her pocket.

Sonja said, "If there's anything I can do to help, just stop by the bakery. It's over on Rue de Medicis, not far from where I met you. We don't actually open until seven, but every morning we start baking at three. I live in an apartment just above the bakery, and if I'm not in the store, I'm probably upstairs. Really, if I can help with anything, just let me know."

"I'll do that," said Claire, "Thanks."

Helen looked deeply into Claire's eyes, and took her hand in both of her own. "You know," she said, "I hope you do stay in Paris. You can't live life in fear. Sure, stuff happens, but you have to have faith that it will all work out in the end, and just go on. My mother used to say, 'Enjoy life while you can, because first thing you know you're old and you can't do things anymore.' And she was right. It's the whole 'carpe diem' thing."

"Amen to that," said Roshni.

"I second that," said Sonja.

Helen nodded once, then released Claire's hand and turned to Peter. "See, Peter, I'm smarter than I look!"

He rolled his eyes. "Yeah, but how hard is that?"

"Hey!" exclaimed Helen, "Not nice!" She scowled at him with feigned insult.

"Enough of all this doom and gloom," Roshni said. "Have you seen any of the sights?"

"Just Notre Dame. And the Luxembourg Gardens."

"Well, you've got to go to the Louvre," said Sonja. "And, of course, the Eiffel Tower. But don't go at night. There are too many hawkers at night harassing people to buy their cheap souvenirs."

"Sacré-Coeur is my favorite place," said Roshni. "The basilica is beautiful, and it sits on a hill in Montmartre. It's built in a different style than most other cathedrals, and looks more like a mosque, with big domes on top instead of the usual spires. It's made of a stone that's pure white, and it always reminds me of a dollop of whipped cream plopped on the hill."

"There's a great story about why Sacré-Coeur was built," said Helen. "When the Franco-Prussian War broke out in 1870, two Catholic French businessmen promised to build a church if Paris was spared invasion by the Prussians. It seems to have worked, because even though Paris suffered a four month siege, it was never actually invaded."

"Not invaded in *that* war, at least," Sonja said bitterly. "Paris always seems to be a prime target for invading armies. I mean, really…how many times have the Germans invaded over the years?"

"There's another great myth about Sacré-Coeur," said Peter. "During WWII, thirteen bombs are supposed to have fallen right around Sacré-Coeur, but miraculously not a soul was injured." He held his hands palms out and shook them, eyes wide-open, eyebrows bobbing up and down. "Woooooooooo!"

"Stop that!" said Helen, punching him in the arm. "God'll get you for that!"

Sonja said, "Have you heard about the *Cimetière du Père Lachaise*?"

Claire shook her head.

"It's probably the most famous cemetery in Paris. The final 'home of the stars.' Lots of celebrities are buried there: Jim Morrison, Oscar Wilde, Edith Piaf... Sundays are busy for us, but if you're free on Monday, I'd love to take you. It's kind of fun to wander around and hob nob with the rich and famous, even if they are dead." Sonja grinned.

"I'd love to, thanks!"

"Where are you staying?"

Claire wrote down her address and cell phone number and gave it to Sonja.

"How about if I pick you up at your apartment at 9:00?"

"That would be wonderful," said Claire.

Roshni looked at her watch. "It's getting late, and I should be going." She stood up and took Claire's hand in both of hers. "Claire, it was really nice meeting you."

Peter said, "We should be going, too." He and Helen stood.

"It was great meeting all of you." Claire smiled.

"Do you need to go, too, Claire?" Sonja asked as the others made their way across the restaurant toward the door. "I'm happy to stay for a while longer if you are."

"Sure, why not?"

Sonja caught the waiter's eye, and when he came over she ordered two glasses of cognac.

"So, Claire, everyone else has said why they came to Paris. What about you?"

The waiter returned with two tulip-shaped glasses of cognac, set them down on the table, and left.

"*Merci*," Sonja said to the waiter as he left. She cradled the bowl of the glass in the palm of her hand and gently swirled it, allowing the liquid to slowly warm.

"When we first met, you said you needed some time on your own, that you just got out of a relationship. Care to expand on that?" Sonja smiled and took a small sip of cognac, then continued to rotate the snifter.

Claire leaned back in her chair, watching the amber liquid as she gently swirled her own cognac. She was silent for a few moments, thinking. Did she want to get into it all?

Sonja quickly added, "I don't want to pry. If you don't want to talk about it, that's fine."

"No, it's ok. It might do me good." Claire smiled, taking a sip of her drink. The cognac was smooth and warmed her throat as she swallowed.

"My partner and I broke up. Actually, we didn't 'break up'; she dumped me after seventeen years of being together. I felt like I needed some time on my own to think about my life and what happened."

"I'm really sorry. Did she say why she wanted out?"

"I'm an attorney, and I've been working for the same firm for about six years. I've heard a rumor that they're considering making me a partner, which would be wonderful and mean a huge increase in my salary. So I've really been putting in long hours for the past year, working late, going in early, you know…trying to impress them and show them that I'd be a good addition to the firm. Kristine resented that I was spending so much time working, and said she felt like a widow. But she's a nurse and worked weekends a lot, too. So even when I had a Saturday off, she might be at the hospital. Didn't seem fair to me. Anyhow, I guess she finally had enough. She said she wanted more out of life than that, and kicked me out of our house."

Sonja nodded slowly, and took another sip of the cognac. She set the snifter down, folded her hands on the table and leaned forward, looking deeply into Claire's eyes.

"Believe me, I completely understand," she began. "Let me tell you a little more about myself. We never had much when I was growing up. My folks lived through the Great Depression, and they worked hard all their lives for the little that we had. My mom would clip coupons and stock up on things when they were on sale. At one point, we had an attic half full of toilet paper because Mom had found a really good sale, and with her coupons, each roll only cost three cents! My dad was a carpenter and would pick up nails that he found on the street, straighten them out, and save them in case he needed them later at home. They taught me to have a good work ethic, and showed me that if you worked hard and lived frugally, you could survive. But growing up, I hated it. I hated being poor, and not being able to afford things, like new clothes before starting school in the fall. I promised myself that when I grew up, I would make lots of money and be able to buy anything that I wanted, whenever I wanted it. And I did."

Sonja took a sip of cognac, and continued. "I used to own a large real estate firm in Boston. I built that baby from the ground up, and worked my ass off. As the business grew I hired other agents to help, but I always felt like I needed to keep my hand in every client's case, looking over the shoulders of the other agents, making sure everything was handled right, and keeping the customers happy. I worked twelve hours a day, seven days a week, did open houses every Sunday for years…you know the drill. I made really good money, but to be honest, that really wasn't what was driving me. It was that American work ethic I learned from Mom and Dad, that I always had to work hard and be in control."

Sonja swirled her glass in silence, thinking for a moment before she went on. "I dated, but I never got married. I had really good friends, but the more I worked, the less I saw of them, and I guess my personality kind of changed over the years. I'll never forget one night I was at some friends' house for dinner, and one of them looked at me with concern and said, "You know, Sonja, you're not as much fun as you used to be. What's happened?" I realized that I had become so focused on work, nose to the grindstone and all, that it was wearing me down. That made me realize I was paying too high a price for my desire to succeed."

"What did you do?"

"That Monday when I went into the office, I told my best realtor that she was now a managing partner, and I took the rest of the day off and went to see a movie. As I walked out of the office, I could feel a huge burden lift off my shoulders. I glanced at my reflection in a store window as I walked by and noticed that my eyebrows were no longer tightly crunched into the scowl that I'd had for years. My face looked soft, and completely at peace. It was one of the best days I ever had."

Claire nodded in understanding.

"Then a year later, I was diagnosed with colon cancer."

"Oh, no! Are you okay?"

Sonja nodded. "Yeah, I'm fine now. I was lucky they caught it at an early stage. But at the time, I thought sure I'd be dead within two years. And I remember thinking about how many years I had wasted struggling to be a success, and for what? Here I was dying, and none of it mattered. My oncologist once told me that 'on their death bed, no one ever wishes that they had spent more time at the office.' She was right. Having cancer really put my life back in perspective, and let me see what's important and what isn't.

In hindsight, it was actually one of the best things that ever happened to me. So when my aunt left me the bakery in Paris a year later, it was a 'no brainer'. I moved to Paris, and have been living my life to the fullest ever since."

Claire swirled her cognac and took another sip, thinking. "So what's your advice for me?"

"Cherish your life and your friends. It will all end too soon, and at the end of your life, you don't want to have any regrets. Don't look back and think, 'Gosh, I wish I would have…' whatever. Enjoy your life and enjoy your friends. And as long as you can financially survive, what will it matter in a hundred years whether you drove a Ford or a Tesla?"

Claire was silent for a few minutes, contemplating her Cognac. She said, "So you think I should tell the firm I'm not interested in being a partner?"

"No, not if you enjoy the work. Just be yourself, but keep a balance in your life between your home life and work. If the firm has any sense, they'll recognize your wisdom in doing so. And if they don't see it, screw them. Find another job." Sonja grinned. "I know…easier said than done."

Claire returned the smile. "That's for sure. But you're probably right."

"And about Kristine? My advice is that you need to talk to her. Tell her you're sorry that you've been so focused on work and ignored the love that the two of you shared. If she was important to you, if you felt like she was 'the one', do whatever it takes to make the relationship work. In the long run, relationships are so much more important than work is."

Claire slowly nodded. She drained the last sip of her cognac and set down her glass. "Thanks for the advice." She smiled. "I mean it. I'm glad we talked."

"Me, too." Sonja looked at her watch. "Now it really is getting late, and I have to be up in three hours to go to work." She stood up. "I'm so glad you came tonight, Claire."

*

It was late by the time Claire got home. She had thoroughly enjoyed the evening, enjoyed talking with everybody and really appreciated Sonja's advice about life and what's important in it. Should she call Kristine now? She looked at her watch. Almost midnight; close to six in the evening in D.C. Kristine was probably home from work by now. She pulled out her cell phone to call, but then paused, thought better of it, and set the phone down on the table. She really was tired, and she should probably be well rested when she launched into this discussion with Kristine. Not to mention the fact that she should plan what she was going to say, and how to say it. But she knew Sonja was right; she needed to talk to Kristine. She nodded decisively to herself; I'll get a good night's sleep, and call her tomorrow.

CHAPTER FIVE

Claire slept well for the first time since she had arrived in Paris. She awoke early, the pale pink light of dawn streaming through her window. She threw on her sweats and went out for a jog. It must have rained during the night, and she filled her lungs with cool morning air that still had that sweet, fresh smell of fallen rain. The sky was robin's egg blue, with a few puffy white clouds scuttling across. It looked like it was going to be another warm, beautiful day.

She passed workmen on scaffolding repairing the stone face of a building, dust coating their clothes and faces. She was delighted to see that some of the old craftsmanship from the 1600s had survived into the twenty first century. She ran past other men who were unloading trucks to deliver beer and soft drinks to restaurants. All of the men that she passed looked like rough, no-nonsense kinds of hard working guys, and she hoped that if she ran into the bearded man again, guys like these would all come to her defense. A woman friend of hers had briefly lived in Paris and had told Claire she had been concerned about her personal safety when she was out walking alone at night. One evening, her friend heard a woman scream on the street in front of her apartment, and she immediately heard apartment doors open and the running of footsteps. Her friend looked out her window just in time to see some of her male neighbors burst out onto the street, pull the woman away from her assailant, and proceed to beat the crap out of the guy. Apparently, chivalry was still alive and well in Paris.

Claire jogged across Boulevard Saint-Michel and entered the Jardin du Luxembourg. A scruffy middle-aged homeless man was bent over a garbage can, digging through it, pulling out half eaten sandwiches and pastries and placing them in a crumpled paper sack. A ghost gray pit bull lay on the ground next to him, vigilant in defense of his master, warily following Claire with his eyes as she ran by. She tried not to make eye contact with the dog or do anything it might think was threatening, and was relieved when she got past him without any problems.

It was too early for many people to be out in the gardens. Dew still kissed the grass, and the enthusiastic chirp of birds and the distant hum of traffic were the only sounds she heard. She made the loop of the gardens and headed back to her apartment, stopping at a patisserie to pick up some fresh pastries.

When she got back home, she put on a pot of coffee, showered and threw on shorts and a tank top. She poured herself a cup of coffee and took her pastry out to the balcony to eat breakfast. The café across the street was open, a few patrons sitting at the outdoor tables with their coffee and newspapers. She glanced up at the apartments across the way and saw the older French man out on his balcony. His eyes met hers, and he smiled and gave a little finger wave. She returned the smile and wave. She finished her coffee and pastry, went back into the kitchen, rinsed out her dishes, and put them away. She saw that she was almost out of fresh fruit, and the baguette that she had bought 3 days earlier was getting stale. She pulled her shopping bag out of a kitchen drawer, locked the apartment, and walked to the grocery store.

*

There were still a few wispy clouds in the azure sky, and the sun felt good on her face as she walked along. She was surprised by how free and unburdened she felt, and was actually happy. She felt like she had finally put Suzie and the bearded man behind her, and was looking forward to enjoying Paris and all that it had to offer. Kristine was right; Claire had wanted to go to Paris ever since she was a little girl. Her mother used to read her the children's books about Madeline and all of her adventures in Paris, and she used to dream about following in her footsteps and having her own adventures. She smiled to herself. Well, Suzie and the bearded man certainly weren't the types of adventures she had in mind when she was a child.

She entered the grocery store and grabbed a shopping basket, then walked to the dairy case at the rear of the store. She picked up some milk and yogurt, and headed to the fruit display. After selecting a few plums, grapes and peaches, she made her way to the bakery section. She gently squeezed the baguettes in their paper sleeves and put a fresh, crunchy loaf in her basket. After picking out a nice bottle of red wine, she went to the checkout aisle. The same clerk who had checked her out three days ago was at the cash register, but this time when Claire said "*Bon jour*," the clerk smiled and replied, "*Bon jour, madame*." Baby steps, Claire told herself.

She returned home and put the groceries away. She grabbed her tourist book and sat on the couch, thumbing through, trying to decide where to go this morning and what to see. She finally decided she'd take Roshni's advice and go to Sacré-Coeur. She pulled out her Metro map and figured out how to get to the basilica in the Montmartre region of Paris. Claire was feeling pretty proud of herself for how comfortable she was with the Parisian subway system. Not that much different from D.C.'s, but still…

*

She walked to the Metro station at St. Michel-Notre Dame and bought a book of Metro tickets from the vending machine. She hopped on the RER B northbound train, then got off at Gare du Nord and switched to the number 4 line toward Porte de Clignancourt. She got off the subway at the Château-Rouge Metro station in the Montmartre neighborhood of Paris.

Montmartre used to be the "artsy" area of Paris, where Salvador Dali, Picasso, and Claude Monet spent a lot of time. Claire had read in her tourist book that even today, many artists set up their easels on the street just below Sacré-Coeur and painted. She read that Montmartre is also the home of the Moulin Rouge, made famous by its scantily clad cancan dancers. This was also the "red light" district known as the "*Pigalle*", mispronounced as "pig alley" by American soldiers in WWII.

Claire walked up the cement stairs from the subway to the street level. When she emerged from the underground, she felt like she was in a different city. Gone were the sweet little old Parisian ladies with their Yorkies on leashes and the businessmen in silk suits. Instead, most of the people on the street looked like African immigrants. There was a tall, thin African man selling peanuts and roasted corn on the cob on the sidewalk, old cornhusks and peanut shells scattered around his stand. Many African men were just hanging around on the sidewalk, smoking cigarettes and not doing anything in particular or going anywhere. She felt a little uncomfortable at first, but then remembered she had read the area was actually quite safe, at least during the day.

Claire pulled out her tourist map of Paris and compass and got her bearings. She headed up the hill on Rue Custine, past *tabac* shops and fruit stands selling African plums and melons. She strolled past dimly lit bars, low rock and roll music wafting out through the open doors. After a few blocks, she could see the dome of Sacré-Coeur high on a hill peeking over the buildings, and climbed a steep, switch-backing staircase toward the basilica.

When she reached the top of the stairs, she could understand why Roshni loved Sacré-Coeur. Its rounded domes and Byzantine architecture gave the basilica more of an Eastern look, rather than the standard Gothic design of so many other cathedrals. Sacré-Coeur is pure white, made of travertine stone. This stone releases calcite when the rain hits it, and it is the calcite that has kept the basilica a pristine white for over a hundred years.

Claire walked to the broad, marbled terrace in front of the church. The view of Paris was spectacular, and in the distance she could just barely see the Eiffel Tower. The morning sun kissed the side of her face, and below her was a broad sloping expanse of grass, flanked on either side by steep stone staircases leading up to the basilica. An ornate carousel was on a plaza beyond the foot of the stairs.

She entered the basilica through tall bronze doors. Marble columns and archways met her, with stained glass windows high on opposing walls. A marble floor with enamel mosaics lay in front of the altar, and a gold, blue, and white mosaic of Jesus, a heart of gold in His chest, formed the domed ceiling above the alter.

Claire strolled through the church, admiring the artwork and statuary. She sat in a pew and savored the peace, silent except for the hushed whispers of a handful of others in the basilica. After a few minutes of solitude, Gregorian chants began to softly echo through the stillness of the church. Claire was suddenly consumed with a calm she had never felt before as the music soothed her to the core, and it was so beautiful that it made the hairs stand up on the back of her neck. She took a deep sigh, and felt all of the tension leave her body. Gone were her concerns about Suzie and the bearded man. She sat, alone amongst the crowd in the church, and reflected on her life.

She thought about Kristine and how she would broach the subject of their relationship when she called. Claire had never loved anyone the way that she loved Kristine, and she had to do whatever it took to make things right between them again. Sonja was right; relationships were the most important things in life, and she had to fix theirs. Her job had to come a distant second.

After several minutes, she knew what she was going to say to Kristine. She sighed, smiling contentedly, then stood up and walked through the front door of the basilica and back to the stairway behind the church. As she started to descend the stairs, she suddenly felt isolated, and realized that there was no one else around. A twinge of concern crawled up the back of her neck, but she willed it away. She continued down the steps, and half way down she felt eyes watching her. She turned, and at the top of the stairs stood the same bearded man from the other day in his white linen robe, staring at her. He began coming down the steps behind her.

73

Claire quickly descended the stairs and turned the corner onto Rue Custine. She darted into a tiny minimart and ducked behind a magazine stand, furtively watching the street through the front window. After a few minutes, the bearded man walked past without even a glance toward the store. Claire heaved a sigh of relief, waited several more minutes, then walked to the door and peeked outside. The bearded man was nowhere to be seen. She hurried down the hill toward the Chateau Rouge Metro station, past the street vendors, and into the cool subterranean depths of the underground. She glanced around…still no sign of the bearded man.

She followed the signs for the Metro purple line #4 going toward Mairie de Montrouge. A large cluster of people stood near the edge of the platform, waiting for the train. The electronic monitor above the platform showed that line 4 would be arriving in 2 minutes. Rather than joust with the other people waiting to climb on board the train from the center of the platform, she moved to the end of the platform right by the tunnel and stood near a cement column.

She saw the headlight of the train in the distance down the tunnel, and felt a gust of wind as it approached. At the same time, she was suddenly grabbed from behind, strong arms encircling her body. The smell of body odor was almost overpowering. She wriggled and struggled to get free, but the man held her tightly against himself. She screamed, but the sound was swallowed by the roar of the rapidly approaching train. Suddenly, like a switch had been thrown in her brain, she'd had enough. Suzie's death, the break in at the apartment, the bearded man, the police…all of it boiled over into an uncontrollable, adrenaline fueled rage. Claire frantically squirmed, drew her left arm forward, then with all her might drove her elbow backwards into her assailant's chest. His arms flew wide as he stumbled backwards, and he cried out as he fell into the path of the oncoming train. A woman screamed.

The train came to a stop at the platform, its undercarriage smeared with blood, the man's body a mangled mass of flesh and cloth on the tracks. Claire stepped behind the cement column and leaned her back against it, eyes closed, breathing hard, trying to stay out of sight of the crowd as it rushed to the edge of the platform, gaping at the carnage. Had anyone seen her? Did they see what had happened? She stepped away from the column and, without even looking toward the track, quickly made her way to the exit stairs.

She climbed up to the street level, her breath coming in gasps, and looked around. She spotted a nearby bench and went over to it, her legs buckling under her as though someone had suddenly pushed the backs of her knees. Street vendors selling souvenir trinkets approached her, but she waved them off. Her brow was dotted with perspiration, and her hand shook as she wiped the sweat away. Take it easy, she told herself. Just take it easy. It wasn't my fault. Well, maybe it was, but I had to do it, I had to get away, somehow. I certainly didn't mean to kill the guy. Do they have surveillance cameras in the subway? Is there a recording of what I did? She rubbed her fists into her eyes, trying to erase the image of the bloody carnage beneath the train. She ran her fingers through her hair and slowly shook her head. Shit, shit, shit.

She stayed on the bench for several minutes, willing herself to breathe slowly, forcing herself to try to relax, to compose herself. She looked around. Everything seemed so normal on the street. These people had no idea about what had just happened. Let's keep it that way, she thought. I need to look as if nothing is wrong.

She heard the repetitive, two toned "wah, wah" of a European siren approaching. A police car came into view, its blue and red lights flashing as it pulled up to the Metro entrance. In its wake was an ambulance. It came to a stop behind the police car, and two paramedics unloaded a gurney and carried it down the stairs. Time to go, she thought, but how do I get home without using this train? She pulled out her Metro map and studied it, checked her compass, then got up and walked down Boulevard Barbes toward Gare du Nord. It was a long walk, but she felt it would help her clear her head.

Passersby glanced at her on the street, and she was certain that they could see right through her, see what had just happened, see that she had just killed a man, see her guilt. Ridiculous, she thought. She mentally shook herself. When she got to Gare du Nord, she took the subway back to the Latin Quarter, and then made her way home.

*

Once inside her apartment, she locked the door behind her and collapsed on the couch. She sat, still stunned, unsure what to do next. She looked at her watch. Twelve thirty. Six thirty in the morning in D.C. She picked up the phone, and dialed. Kristine answered on the second ring.

"Kristine, it's me. Sorry to bother you again, but…" she paused, not sure what to say.

"But, what?" Kristine said with impatience. "I have to leave for work in a few minutes, Claire, so make it fast."

"I just killed a man." She ran her hand through her hair, her eyes filling with tears.

"Holy shit, Claire!" she exclaimed, suddenly not so concerned about leaving for work. "What happened?"

Claire told her about being followed from Sacré-Coeur and the struggle at the Metro station.

"Have you talked to the police?"

"Hell, no! They already think I killed Suzie. They'd think I was a fucking serial killer!"

Kristine was silent for a moment as she digested what had happened. "Well, I guess the good news is that you won't be followed anymore."

"And aside from that, Mrs. Kennedy, how did you like Dallas?" she said, her voice dripping with sarcasm.

"I'm serious," Kristine said. "You're finally free to enjoy Paris. Nobody's after you now. It's all over. Think about it." There was a pause, and then she continued, "You've always been good at compartmentalizing things and being rational. Put Suzie and all of this other crap in a room in your brain, lock the door, and throw away the key."

Claire was silent for a moment, mulling over what Kristine had said. Maybe she was right. "I had dinner last night with some real nice ex-pats, and I told them about what's been going on. They thought I should just try to enjoy Paris, too. One woman owns a bakery near my apartment called American Pie. She's going to take me to the cemetery tomorrow to see where Jim Morrison and Oscar Wilde are buried."

"There you go!"

She chuckled grimly. "Of course, all of that was arranged before I became a mass murderer."

They talked for a few more minutes before Kristine said, "I really do need to leave for work, Claire. Keep me posted, ok, kiddo? And really…try to have a good time."

*

Claire hung up the phone and took a deep, cleansing breath, locking her fingers behind her head and slouching down on the couch. Maybe Kristine was right. The bearded man was gone, and nobody was stalking her now. Whatever had been going on, it was over now. But still…she just killed a man. Not really her fault, though. At home, it would have been called "self-defense", or even "justifiable homicide." Was it the same in France? If Inspector Girard knew what had happened, would he arrest her? Or would he let her go without any charges being filed? She didn't know, and she really didn't want to find out.

She got up and poured herself a glass of wine and stepped out onto the balcony. The old man across the way was out on his balcony watching the world go by. He and Claire made eye contact.

"*Bon jour, madame!*" he shouted, broadly waving.

Claire smiled despite herself. "*Bon jour, monsieur!*" and waved back.

Still with a soft smile on her face, she took a sip of her wine and went back to her couch. Seems like a nice enough old guy, she thought. Or maybe he's just a lecherous old man. She chuckled to herself. Even if he was, who cares? She suddenly realized that despite what had happened in the subway, she actually did feel relief, even free, for the first time since she had arrived in Paris. She smiled to herself. Maybe everything really would be okay.

She decided to try to relax and spend the afternoon enjoying some art. She was in Paris, after all. Probably not enough time to go to the Louvre; she'd heard a person could spend days there admiring all of the paintings and sculptures on its four floors. Instead, she decided to go to the Orsay museum. It was within walking distance of her apartment, and it was a beautiful day. The stroll would do her good, she thought.

*

Claire spent the entire afternoon with Rodin, Monet, and Cézanne. She stayed at the Orsay until it closed at 6:00, and was one of the last people to leave the museum. She was famished, and once she got back to the Latin Quarter she stopped at an elegant restaurant and took a seat at one of the outdoor tables. A middle-aged waiter came by and handed her a menu. Everything looked so good, but expensive. Who cares, she thought. I'm on vacation, and I deserve to treat myself after everything that has happened. She ordered lobster thermidor and a glass of white wine, then leaned back with her wine and watched the people passing by. She was happy, and savored her food. By the time the check came, she was pooped and ready for a good night's sleep. And she realized that the best part of the afternoon was that she hadn't seen any more bearded men in linen robes. Finally, she could enjoy Paris!

*

She was up early, went for a run, and came home and showered. She had breakfast and her coffee out on the balcony. The older man across the street wasn't out on his porch; maybe he had a hot date last night, she thought, and is still cuddling in bed. She smiled at the thought. "Enjoy life while you can", isn't that what Helen's mom used to say? Pretty good advice.

A little before 9:00 she went into the bedroom and dug through her suitcase, finally pulling out a small, metallic red camera, and an instruction manual. Slipping the camera and manual in her pocket, she locked up the apartment and headed out.

Claire glanced up and down the street as she waited for Sonja. Half way down the block, she saw that same green Peugeot that she had seen the other day. Two men were in the car, but she couldn't see what they looked like. Must be waiting for someone.

On the dot of 9:00, Sonja drove up in her little red bug-like Fiat. Claire hopped in, and off they went.

"The cemetery is huge, more than a hundred acres," Sonja said as they threaded their way through the congested Parisian traffic. "They don't like to have cars in the cemetery, so we'll have to park on the street and walk in."

As they drove, Claire pulled the camera out of her pocket and began fiddling with it, frequently consulting the instruction manual.

"New camera?" asked Sonja.

"Yeah. I just got it before I left home. I haven't used it much this trip, and I'm still trying to figure it out."

"It's a very pretty color."

They parked on Boulevard de Menilmontant, and strolled to a minimarket across the street from the cemetery. They bought two tourist maps showing the final resting places of some of the more famous residents, and then headed for the cemetery's gate. Claire walked a few yards into the *Cimetière du Père Lachaise* and stopped, gazing around in astonishment. She had never seen a cemetery like this. Rather than the rolling, open grassy hills so common in American cemeteries, the *Cimetière du Père Lachaise* was almost solidly packed with graves. Mausoleums made of massive stone blocks with ornate metal doors stood nearly shoulder-to-shoulder on either side of the cobblestone roads crisscrossing the cemetery. Flat grave ledgers and above ground crypts, large enough to encase a casket, were interspersed between the mausoleums, and huge, ornate tombstones reached heavenwards. The cemetery monuments were so tightly crammed together, there was less than a twelve-inch gravel gap between many of them. With the quaint cobblestone lanes winding between the house-like tombs, Claire got the creepy impression that it was a village of the dead. There were even street signs identifying each of the cobblestone roads.

"Where shall we start?" asked Sonja.

They consulted their maps, and started to explore. The cemetery felt pretty deserted, and they only came across a handful of other visitors as they wandered around. They found their way to the graves of Jim Morrison and Chopin, and were in front of Edith Piaf's raised grave ledger when Sonja pointed off to the left and said, "I'm going over this way to Gertrude Stein's and Alice B. Toklas' graves."

"OK," said Claire. "I'll be there in a second. I just want to take a picture of this tomb. Kristine loves Edith Piaf's music."

Sonja walked down the cobblestone lane and turned the corner.

Claire pulled out her camera and held it in front of her face, trying to frame a good picture of the grave marker.

She felt someone come up behind her, grab her left arm and press something against her right side.

"You scream, you die," whispered a man with a Middle Eastern accent.

Claire froze, dropping her camera. Her eyes grew wide with terror. "What do you want? Let me go!"

"Move." The man pressed the knife a little harder against her side, and guided her by her arm down the cobblestone lane.

Claire repeated, "What do you want?"

"Shut up." He prodded her onward with the knife.

They made their way down the road and turned a corner. The man suddenly stopped, tightening his grip on Claire's arm. A tour group of perhaps a dozen people stood clustered around a grave, the tour guide holding a closed umbrella at arm's length high above her head as she rattled off something in Italian.

In an instant, Claire knew what she had to do, as it might be the only chance she had. She suddenly wrested her arm away from the man and ran, ran as fast as she could down the road past the tour group as they looked on with curiosity. She darted in between two mausoleums and wound her way between the tightly packed graves. She shot a glance over her shoulder; the man was following thirty feet behind. She ducked her head down and dashed through the maze of towering tombstones and mausoleums. She was breathing hard after several minutes of weaving her way through the labyrinth of grave monuments, her lungs feeling like they were about to explode. She collapsed down behind a large tombstone, leaning her head against the marble monument, and closed her eyes, gasping for breath. She tried to force herself to breathe quietly as she struggled to catch her breath, not wanting the man to hear her. She opened her eyes and held her breath for a moment and listened; the only sounds that came to her were the birds in the branches overhead. She took a deep cleansing breath and closed her eyes. Now what?

Sonja stood in front of Gertrude Stein's grave and glanced at her watch; it had been at least ten minutes since she had left Claire. Where was she? Did she get lost? She retraced her steps back to Edith Piaf's gravesite. No Claire. Then she noticed a metallic red object on the ground, and went over to pick it up. Claire's camera. What the heck was going on?

After several minutes, Claire finally caught her breath. What now, she wondered. Do I try to find Sonja? Or do I get up and make a run for the gate and get the hell out of here and away from that guy? Well, I can't stay sitting here forever, she thought.

She drew herself to her feet and turned around, looking over the top of the tombstone. The man was standing on the other side of the granite grave marker, looking at her straight in the face, just inches away. He quickly grabbed her arm before she had a chance to run, and put his knife to her throat.

"Are you done playing hide and seek?" he asked, grinning, tobacco-stained teeth leering at her. "Move."

His knife once again pressed against her side, his other hand tightly gripping her arm, as they made their way to the main gate of the cemetery. A sage green Peugeot was waiting. The man opened the rear door and threw her in the back seat of the Peugeot, climbing in after her. He grabbed her hair and pulled her head back, and placed the knife against her throat as the car sped off.

"What do you want? Let me go!"

"We know you have it, and we want it back," the man said.

"I don't know what you're talking about. I don't have anything!" Claire was terrified. She suddenly realized that they hadn't put a blindfold on her, or made any effort to cover their faces. They don't care, she thought. They're going to kill me. She could feel the sharp edge of the knife pressing into her flesh just below her chin, above her Adam's apple.

"We know Suzie gave it to you. You will tell us where it is, or you will end up like her." The man smiled, the rank smell of body odor filling the car. He moved the knife to her side, the tip poking through her shirt just below her ribs, and released her hair. "You don't want to die, do you?"

The car raced down Boulevard de Menilmontant.

"She didn't give me anything!" Claire protested. "And she wasn't my friend. I'd just met her on the plane. You've got the wrong person!" Claire looked into the man's eyes, and saw cold hatred looking back.

"I don't think Suzie would have lied. She didn't want to tell us about you at first, but she finally realized the futility of not talking." He smiled again, and chuckled. "It only took a little encouragement from us."

Claire remembered what must have been cigarette burns on Suzie's chest, and felt sick to her stomach. Her hands were free, but she knew she couldn't move without immediately being stabbed by the knife against her side.

The car sped down the street, weaving through traffic. They were approaching a roundabout at Place de la Nation when the driver suddenly turned and looked at the man in the back seat, and said something in Arabic. The car entered the roundabout and the swarm of traffic. Claire looked to the right just in time to see a large delivery truck come barreling down a main arterial, right toward them. The truck's horn blared as it plowed into the Peugeot's passenger's door, spinning the car around 360 degrees, then it stopped. Claire and the man with the knife were both thrown to the right side of the car with the impact, then rebounded back to the left. Claire's head smacked hard against her window, and shooting stars danced before her eyes. The man with the knife had blood running from his nose, his head leaning against his window. Claire saw that the knife had fallen to the floor, but the man seemed too dazed to notice. She opened her door, burst out of the car, and ran down the street. She quickly glanced back and saw the truck driver get out of his vehicle, his arms waving about in the air and shouting something in French at the driver, as a small crowd gathered around the car. The other driver stayed in his car, and suddenly backed the Peugeot up. The crowd jumped out of the way as the car sped off, the truck driver shaking his fist and yelling at the retreating Peugeot.

Claire ran, not sure if the car was following her. She rounded a corner and stopped, bent over, her hands on her knees, gasping for breath. She suddenly became aware of a searing pain just below her ribs. She touched her side, and felt something sticky and warm. She looked at her fingers...blood. She instantly felt light-headed, and the world went dark.

CHAPTER SIX

"*Madame? Madame?*"

Claire opened her eyes. She was flat on her back on the sidewalk. A young man knelt at her side, and a small knot of people peered down at her. She started to sit up but fell back, too dizzy and light headed to stay up.

"*Comment allez vous?*" the man asked.

Claire closed her eyes. "I don't speak French," she said, for what seemed like the hundredth time in the past four days.

"How do you feel?" the man asked in English.

Claire could hear the distant "wah wah" of an approaching siren. "I've been better."

She tried to sit up again.

"Stay down until help comes," the man said, gently pushing her back down. "*Vous avez une coupe.*" He pointed to her side, then looked up to the sky, thinking. "Ummm…you have a cut."

The ambulance arrived, and two paramedics got out. They were both young, no older than their mid-twenties, one a man and the other a woman. The crowd parted to let them through. They came to where Claire was lying on the sidewalk and knelt down.

"*Bon jour, madame,*" the male paramedic said, smiling reassuringly. "*Comment allez vous?*"

"I'm sorry, I don't speak French." Claire thought that maybe she should just get a tattoo of that phrase on her arm so all she'd have to do is roll up her sleeve, show it, and be done with it. Save a lot of time, she thought.

"You have been hurt?" the male paramedic said. The woman attendant took a penlight from her breast pocket and shined it in one of Claire's eyes, then the other.

Claire nodded. "I was in a car accident. And was stabbed." She pointed to her right side.

The man gently pulled up her blouse and looked at the wound. He pursed his lips and shook his head. "I will need to start a…" he tapped the bend in his elbow, then turned to his colleague and asked, "*Qu'est-ce que c'est?*"

"Intravenous," she said.

"Ah, *oui*, intravenous."

"Okay."

The man rolled up her left sleeve and started an IV while the woman paramedic gently felt Claire's neck, then put a neck brace on her. She cautiously prodded at the wound on Claire's side and smiled. "It is good," she said, "not too deep." She put a piece of gauze over the wound and covered it with paper tape. She examined the bleeding bump on the side of Claire's head and dabbed at it with a clean piece of gauze. No fresh bleeding.

"It is okay," the woman said, pointing to her head.

Once the IV was in place, the paramedics bundled her up, put her on a stretcher, slid her into the back of the ambulance, and sped off.

They wove their way through traffic, the woman paramedic frequently checking Claire's blood pressure and shining a light in her eyes, murmuring what she assumed were soothing words in French. Soon, they turned into a driveway and Claire saw a sign that said, "*Groupe*

Hospitalier de la Pitie Salpetriere" through the ambulance window. The ambulance backed up to an entrance, the "beep beep beep" of reverse cutting the silence, and stopped. The driver opened the back door, and they wheeled her into the ER.

There were twenty or thirty people in various degrees of distress waiting in the Emergency Room. Some had bloody bandages wrapped around an arm or leg. One young man had a bowl on his lap, his face mere inches above it, vomiting with vigor. An older woman held an ice pack to her forehead; her head was leaned back against the wall, her eyes closed.

A nurse in green scrubs met the paramedics, exchanging a few words with the ambulance team. They wheeled Claire into an examining room and brought her gurney up alongside another stretcher. They wadded up a section of the sheet beneath Claire, and with an "*un, deux, trios*" they lifted her off the gurney and onto the other stretcher. The ambulance team stripped and crumpled up the bedding from their gurney. The male paramedic called "*Bon chance, madame!*" over his shoulder, and left.

"*Bon jour, madame*" the nurse said, smiling. "*Comment vous appelez-vous?*"

"Sorry, I don't speak French."

"What is your name?"

"Claire McKenna."

"You are American?"

"Yes."

"Do you have your passport?"

"I don't have it with me." Talk to Inspector Girard about that, Claire thought bitterly.

"How do you feel?"

"Okay, I guess."

"Is there someone you would like us to call? A friend?"

Claire shook her head at first, but then said, "Actually, yes." Claire pulled her wallet out of her pants pocket, and took out Peter's business card. "This is my friend at the Embassy. Could you please call him?"

"Of course." The nurse slid the card into her pocket. She pulled back the sheet, peeled off the bandage and looked at the wound in Claire's side. "This will need…" She paused, thinking, then mimicked sewing something.

"Stitches?"

"*Oui*," the nurse said, nodding. "Stitches. The doctor will be in soon."

The nurse hooked Claire up to a heart monitor and stepped out. Maybe ten minutes later, a woman in a white coat stepped into the room. She was middle aged with wavy brown hair pulled up and back, away from her face. She had intelligent blue eyes, and wore simple pearl earrings. She reminded Claire of Margaret Thatcher. A stethoscope was draped around her neck.

"*Bon jour*," she said. "You do not speak French?"

Claire shook her head. "Sorry."

"It is not a problem. I did some of my training in New York, and I speak English. I am Dr. Benoît. Can you tell me what happened?"

"I was in the *Cimetière du Père Lachaise* when a man came up behind me, put a knife to my side, and kidnapped me. We ended up in a car accident and I was able to get away, but I guess I got stabbed." Claire pointed to her right side.

"Let me have a look." The doctor pulled the sheet back and carefully removed the dressing. She felt around the wound, gently pulling it apart to see how deep it was. Claire winced.

"Sorry." Dr. Benoît put the dressing and the sheet back in place. "It is not too deep, but it will need stitches. You hit your head, too?"

She nodded. The doctor pulled a penlight from her coat pocket and shined it into Claire's eyes. Then she examined the left side of her head. "You lost consciousness?"

She nodded. "For a few minutes, I guess."

"Any nausea? Dizziness? Headache?"

She shook her head.

"I do not think it is anything serious," Dr. Benoît said. "You have a concussion. You should feel fine in a week or two." She paused, and grew serious. "We are required to notify the police about stabbings and kidnappings. They should be here soon to talk to you."

Claire nodded. "Okay."

She smiled. "I will be back in a few minutes to sew you up. After the police have come and talked to you, you should be ready to go home." The doctor stepped out, leaving Claire alone.

It had been a long day, and she had to admit that it was nice to know that she was finally safe. She must have dozed off.

"How are you feeling?"

Claire opened her eyes. Peter stood in the doorway, concern etched on his face. She thought he must have come straight from the Embassy, since he was dressed in a dark suit and tie.

"Could be worse. Thanks for coming." She scooted herself higher up into a sitting position on the stretcher, grimacing a little as her wound was stretched. She was relieved to have someone in the ER with her, someone she knew she could count on to help.

"Not a problem," Peter said. He pulled up a folding chair and sat down next to the stretcher. "So, what happened? You were in an accident?"

"I was in the *Cimetière du Père Lachaise* with Sonja. We got separated, and all of a sudden a man grabbed me, put a knife to my side, and kidnapped me. I was able to get away for a few minutes, but then he found me again and dragged me out to the street and threw me in a car. He said they wanted something that I had, something Suzie had given me."

Peter furrowed his brow. "Any idea what he was talking about?"

She shook her head. "I haven't a clue. As we were driving along, a truck smacked into us and I was able to get away. But not before I got cut on my side."

He sat silently for a moment, elbows on his knees, chin resting on his folded hands, thinking.

Claire wondered if she should mention what had happened that morning at Sacré-Coeur. She thought for a minute, debating with herself how much to tell him, then said, "Well, let me just say that I have no idea what it is that they're after. But to be honest, there is a little more to the story than that. Um, I guess I haven't told you everything."

He sat up and raised his eyebrows expectantly.

"Do you remember when we all met Saturday night, I told you and the others about being followed to Notre Dame, and my apartment being broken into?"

He nodded.

"Well, yesterday I took Roshni's advice and went to see Sacré-Coeur. As I was leaving the basilica, I was followed by a bearded Middle Eastern man, the same one who had followed me in the Luxembourg Gardens after I'd found Suzie dead."

"Was it the same man that grabbed you just now?"

"No."

"Would you be able to describe him?"

It sure would be easy to describe what he looked like right now, she thought. A pile of raw hamburger. She shrugged. "It…doesn't really matter now."

He looked at her, confused, and shook his head. "Why not?"

Claire looked at the ceiling, trying to think how to explain it. "Um…here's the deal. From Sacré-Coeur he followed me down to the Metro station. I was waiting for the train and I didn't see him come up behind me. He grabbed me, I struggled and hit him, and…" she bit her lower lip. "…accidentally knocked him into the path of the oncoming train."

"Sweet Jesus!" His eyes grew wide, and he shook his head in disbelief.

She took a deep breath and continued. "I haven't told anybody about that. Well, I did tell my ex-girlfriend, but nobody else." Claire paused. "I'm afraid if the police find out, they'll think I'm a homicidal maniac."

Peter was quiet for a few moments, mulling over what she had told him. "Yeah, probably best not to mention it."

They just looked at each other for a long moment. Finally, he said, "So the guys that nabbed you today…do you think you could describe them?"

She shook her head. "Not really. Bearded, in white robes…nothing specific."

"Well, they obviously know where you live. Do you think it's safe to go back home?"

Her brows knit with concern. "I hadn't thought about that."

Peter cocked his head, thinking. "I bet Sonja would be willing to let you stay with her. She has an extra room. Do you want me to ask her?"

Claire nodded. "Yes, please. That would probably be a good idea. And could you please tell her what happened? She's probably wondering why I disappeared in the cemetery."

Dr. Benoît entered the room, followed by a nurse rolling a small cart.

"Ready?" the doctor asked.

"I'll step out and call Sonja," Peter said, and left the room.

The nurse set the cart next to the bed and drew back Claire's sheet. She pulled up her shirt to expose the bandage, and gently removed the dressing from the wound. The nurse carefully opened the small pack on the cart while Dr. Benoît pulled on sterile gloves.

"Is this your first time in Paris?" she asked.

"Yes," she said. "And probably my last."

The doctor took a folded blue cloth from the pack and draped it over Claire's side, a hole in the cloth surrounding the wound. She then pulled out a six-inch foil pack, bulging at one end. She tore open the foil pack and pulled out a large Q-tip soaked with rust-colored liquid. She dabbed at the wound with the liquid, painting the wound and the surrounding skin with the swab, making increasingly large circular sweeps until they nearly filled the hole in the drape.

"Ah, that would be a shame. Paris is a wonderful city." She tossed the swab into the trash and picked up a syringe from the pack. The nurse wiped off the top of a vial with an alcohol swab, inverted it, and held it out toward the doctor. Dr. Benoît removed the plastic tip from the needle, withdrew the plunger, inserted it into the upside down vial, and injected air into the bottle. She drew liquid into the syringe and pulled the needle out of the vial. The nurse set the vial back down on the tray and left the room.

"What happened to you is not common," Dr. Benoît said. "Please, do not judge the city for what a single man has done."

Or two men, or three men, Claire thought. But still, she had to admit that the doctor was probably right. Maybe she should give Paris a second chance. In about ten years.

"This will sting a little," the doctor said as she injected the anesthetic into Claire's side. After just a few seconds, she couldn't feel a thing around her wound. The doctor picked up a blue paper package the size of a band-aid from the tray, ripped it open, and picked up a hemostat. Using the hemostat like tweezers, she pulled a curved needle out of the pack, a long section of black thread following behind, already attached to the needle. The doctor began to sew up the wound, snipping the thread after each stitch.

"Have you had the chance to see anything in Paris?"

"Not much. Just *Cimetière du Père Lachaise*, Notre Dame and Sacré Coeur." Claire thought she would just as soon forget the cemetery and Sacré Coeur.

"You must see the Eiffel Tower, the Louvre, the Rodin museum...there is so much art, so much beauty." Dr. Benoît snipped the thread on the final suture and set down the scissors and hemostat on the tray. "All done." She smiled as she put a dressing over the wound, and secured it with tape. "Twenty six stitches. I am very good with stitches, so it should not leave a bad scar."

She began cleaning up the used gauze, bandages, and suture material. Just as she was finishing, Inspector Girard stepped into the room.

"We meet again, *madame*," he said to Claire.

Claire looked up at him. There was no warmth in his face, just serious business.

Dr. Benoît looked at Inspector Girard, then turned back to Claire. "I will finish your paperwork, and you should be ready to leave in fifteen minutes." The doctor looked at Inspector Girard, nodded once, said, "*Monsieur*," and left.

Inspector Girard pulled a folding chair up alongside the stretcher and sat down. "I heard you were in an accident, and were kidnapped? Is that correct?"

Claire nodded.

"Please, tell me what happened."

Claire told him the whole story. Almost. She certainly didn't want to mention Sacré Coeur. She told him that the men seemed to be looking for some object, but she had no idea what they were talking about. When she was done, she just looked at Inspector Girard, waiting for his response. He stroked his chin thoughtfully, and leaned back in his chair.

"Interesting. And you have no idea what it is that they wanted?"

She shook her head. "No."

Peter came back into the room and stood behind the policeman. The Inspector briefly glanced at him, and then focused his attention back on Claire. He stared at her for some time without speaking, the room silent except for the rhythmic beeping of her heart monitor. Finally, he said, "A man was killed at the Château-Rouge Metro station yesterday. What can you tell me about that?"

Claire could feel herself wither under his steady gaze, and her face flush. She shot a glance at Peter, who raised his eyebrows and shrugged in an "I don't know" gesture.

"There is no need to lie. We saw you on the surveillance camera at the station." He leaned forward and put his elbows on his knees, his chin resting on his folded hands, his eyes boring into Claire's. "We always seem to catch you on the surveillance camera where someone had been killed."

She was silent, staring at her hands, trying to control her panic, thinking of what to say. "It was self-defense," she began. She could feel perspiration start to bead on her neck and face, and there was a knot deep in her belly. Her chest rose and fell in quiet, shallow breaths. Just take it easy, she thought. She took a deep breath and summoned a surety and self-confidence that she didn't feel, and returned the Inspector's steady gaze. "He had been following me from Sacré Coeur, and he grabbed me." She hesitated for a moment. "I thought he was going to kill me." She always had been a good poker player, and trying to appear calm in this maelstrom that she found herself in was the most important bluff of her life.

Inspector Girard said nothing for what seemed like a long time. Finally, he nodded and leaned back in his chair again. "I understand," he said. "We saw everything that happened." His eyes seemed to soften, and almost showed concern. "Are you going back to your apartment?" he asked.

"I'd really like to get my passport back so I can just go home."

Inspector Girard shook his head. "I'm afraid that is not possible. You are still a suspect in Suzie's murder."

"Seriously?" Claire asked with incredulity.

"I know it is not likely that you killed her, but we must be certain."

Claire shook her head in disbelief. "Well, in that case I guess I'll be staying with a friend in Paris."

He nodded. "That is probably very wise. I would like that address, please."

"I can give it to you," said Peter.

*

It was almost 2:00 by the time Peter and Claire arrived at American Pie. They had stopped by Claire's apartment so she could pack up all of her things, and when they arrived at the bakery Sonja was behind the counter, just finishing up with a customer. A young woman next to Sonja was taking almond pastries from a baking sheet and setting them in the display case.

"Boy, am I glad to see you!" Sonja said, handing her customer his change and pastry. "When I found your camera on the ground in front of Piaf's grave, I started to get worried. Peter told me what happened. Are you okay?"

Claire nodded. "A lot better than it could have been. Only twenty-six stitches; I can live with that. Thanks for letting me stay here."

"Happy to help. Let's get you settled in." Sonja turned to the young woman behind the counter and said something to her in French, and the woman nodded. "It's this way," Sonja said.

They followed Sonja through the kitchen, Peter wheeling the suitcase along behind him. A large table was in the center of the kitchen, residual flour still dusting its perimeter. Cooking utensils hung from hooks over the table, and large baking pans were stacked on the counters around the room.

"There's a surprise waiting for you upstairs," Sonja said over her shoulder as they climbed a narrow staircase at the back of the kitchen, a sly smile on her face. They reached the apartment door, and Sonja opened it.

"Hello, Claire."

CHAPTER SEVEN

Kristine sat on the couch, smiling.

Claire was stunned with disbelief, her mouth gaping open. Was she imagining this? She did have a head injury, after all. No, this was real. "What are you doing here?" She grinned broadly with delight.

Kristine came over and gave her a big hug, the sweet scent of her honeysuckle shampoo filling her nostrils. Claire winced and softly groaned when her side was touched.

Kristine released her and stepped back, her hands still resting on her shoulders, her face clouded with concern. "Oh, geez, I'm sorry. Are you ok?"

She nodded and grinned. "Oh, yeah. It was worth it."

Kristine turned to Peter and extended her hand. "Hi, I'm Kristine. You must be Peter."

He set the suitcase upright on the floor and grasped her hand, smiling. "That I am. Nice to meet you."

"Come on, Peter," Sonja said. "Let's leave these two alone. They've got a lot to talk about. If you need anything, I'll be downstairs." Sonja winked at Claire, then the two of them left, closing the apartment door behind them.

Sonja's apartment was small, but comfortable. A brocade couch was along one wall with a matching wing back chair across from it. Polished cherry wood tables holding small gilded table lamps were on either end of the couch. Several impressionist paintings adorned the walls. Two tall French windows were open, the faint sounds of afternoon traffic drifting through.

Kristine took Claire by the hand. "Come on, let's sit down," she said, leading her to the couch. "Sounds like you've had a hell of a day."

Kristine's blond hair was cut short into a layered bob with long, sweeping bangs. Her eyebrows were knit with concern over her green eyes. Her light-weight, embroidered cream-colored Indian blouse was untucked and fell over her snug blue jeans. Her cheeks were a little flushed. With excitement? With affection? Claire wasn't sure. God, she thought, she looks great.

"I can't believe you're here," Claire said happily.

"Well..." she shrugged, smiling, "after your homicidal attack in the subway, I thought you could use a little emotional support. Little did I know that things would get even worse." Her face clouded with worry. "Are you ok? How's your side?"

Claire pulled up her blouse and showed her the bandage. A small spot of blood had oozed through the dressing. "Twenty six stitches. But it could have been a lot worse."

Kristine shook her head with disbelief and grinned. "You can't be left alone for one minute, can you?"

"Maybe not." Claire smiled. "How on earth did you find me?"

"I went to the apartment first, but you weren't there. Then I remembered you had mentioned the ex-pat who owned American Pie, so I looked up the address on my phone."

"So you _do_ listen to what I say!" she said playfully.

Kristine smiled. "Sometimes, I guess. Anyway, when I got here Sonja told me what had happened at the cemetery this morning, and that you'd be staying with her for a few days."

"Well, thanks for coming. Really. It means a lot to me."

"It's what friends do," she said, shrugging. "And I do still consider us to be friends."

Claire sighed deeply. She really did need to talk to her about their relationship and if they could rebuild their lives, but this certainly wasn't the right time.

"I feel the same way." Claire gave Kristine's hand a little squeeze.

"Ouch!" she cried, withdrawing her hand and rubbing her little finger beneath a small gold ring.

Claire took her hand again and lightly ran her thumb over the two small hearts that were entwined on the ring.

"You're still wearing the ring that I gave you when we moved in together."

She released her hand and self-consciously smiled, fingering the ring with her other hand. "Well, it is a nice ring."

Neither said anything for a moment. Kristine finally broke the silence. "You've got quite the blood stain there," she said, pointing to Claire's blouse. "Why don't you take that blouse off and put it in some cold water? Then would you mind if we took a nap? I couldn't sleep on the plane, and I've been up for…" she looked at her watch, "about thirty two hours. I'm beat. Afterwards, maybe we can get a bite to eat, and then see some sights? I've never been to Paris before, either, you know."

"That would be great." Despite all that had been happening, she couldn't remember when she had been so happy. It felt so right to be with Kristine again. They really did need to talk.

Kristine wheeled Claire's suitcase into the spare bedroom and set it at the foot of the bed. White lace curtains hung over tall French windows, and a pink chenille bedspread covered the queen-sized bed. An oak dresser sat against one wall, and impressionist art adorned the walls.

As Kristine turned down the bed, Claire took off her blouse and put it to soak in cold water. She went back into the bedroom and got undressed, carefully protecting her side. Kristine sat on the bed and slipped off her shoes. They were hot pink running shoes, almost fluorescent.

"Quite the shoes," Claire said, pointing. "Very chic."

She laughed. "They make it a little easier to be seen when I go running in the evening." She slipped off her pants, blouse, and bra, and slid in beneath the covers. Claire crawled in beside her. They looked at each other for a moment, not saying a word. "No funny stuff," Kristine said seriously. "We're just friends, remember?"

Claire couldn't help feeling a little hurt. "Would you at least hold me? Just to comfort an old friend?"

She smiled. "Of course."

She opened her arms and Claire laid her head on her bare breast, her arm encircling Kristine's naked torso. Kristine wrapped her arms around her and cuddled her against her chest. Her breast was as soft as a down pillow and as smooth as velvet. Claire nuzzled against the breast, breathing in the lavender perfume she had always loved, smiling to herself.

Claire sighed. "This is nice. I've really missed this."

Kristine didn't say a word, but Claire could feel her stiffen a little beneath her. She sat up and looked down at her.

"Don't read anything into this," Kristine said. "Let's just enjoy being together as friends for the moment."

Claire smiled, and lay back down on Kristine's breast. "OK by me."

*

When Claire awoke, it was just after three in the afternoon. Sunlight streamed in through the thin curtains. Kristine was softly snoring, mouth gaping open a little. So damned cute, Claire thought.

"Kristine?" Claire whispered.

She stirred and opened her eyes. When she saw Claire, she smiled.

Claire said, "Ready for a late lunch, then the sights of Paris?"

Kristine yawned, and stretched her arms out wide. "Sounds good." She disengaged herself from Claire and swung her legs over the side of the bed, and pulled on her clothes. She sat back on the bed and put on her shoes.

Claire watched her get dressed, enjoying the view. Then she got up and reached for her suitcase.

"Let me get that," Kristine said. She picked up the suitcase and flopped it on the bed.

"Thanks." She began pawing through her packed clothes, searching for a clean blouse to wear. "So, what do you want to see?"

"There's so much to see in Paris, it really doesn't matter where we start. You pick."

Claire thought for a minute. "How about the Eiffel Tower?"

"Sounds like a plan."

"My purse is by the front door," Claire said as she pulled on her pants. "Would you mind getting it? There's a Metro map in one of the pockets. We'll need to see which subway to take." She took a blouse out of the suitcase and gingerly put her arm through the right sleeve.

Kristine walked into the living room and retrieved the purse. She sat on the couch and opened the main section of the bag and rooted around, pulling out Kleenex, lipstick, a pen, some paper… no map. She then unzipped a side pocket and peered in. Her brows furrowed, and she pulled out a tiny, thin piece of rectangular black plastic, about ¼ inch by ½ inch in size.

"Claire?"

"Be there in a minute."

Kristine turned the object over in her hand. On the back were eight short, parallel gold colored strips. "What's this?"

Claire came back into the living room, fastening her belt. "What's what?"

Kristine held it up.

Claire came over and took the object from Kristine and closely examined it. "Oh, shit. That's a data chip. And it's not mine." They looked at each other for a moment in silence. "That must be what they're after."

"What do we do?"

"We'd better ask Sonja how to get to the American Embassy."

*

The American Embassy was just north of Avenue Des Champs Elysées, near the Place de la Concorde on Avenue Gabriel. It was a four-story, cream-colored stone building, with an American flag fluttering above the door. A ten-foot, black wrought iron security fence, with menacing spikes protruding from each spire, surrounded the Embassy. A line of broad-leafed trees ran the length of the building between the fence and the street. Cement barricades surrounded the building, with retractable obstacles across the driveway to prevent access by vehicles. A kiosk for guards was next to the driveway, and two armed Marine guards in their dress blues stood sentry near the gate.

The two women walked toward the entrance. One of the guards walked into the kiosk while the other stood his ground, intently watching them, waiting for them to approach, automatic rifle held at the ready across his body.

"Hello," Claire said to the closest Marine. "My name is Claire McKenna. I'm an American citizen and I'd like to talk to a friend of mine who is an Embassy employee." She reached into her pocket and took out Peter's business card and handed it to the guard. "His name is Peter Bowen. Please tell him it's important."

The guard glanced at the card. "Wait here, please, ma'am." He retreated into the kiosk, picked up a phone and spoke a few words, then came back out to the women. "Mr. Bowen will be out shortly. Please wait here."

"Thank you." Claire raised her eyebrows to Kristine, who smiled.

Aside from the distant traffic on the Avenue Des Champs Elysées behind them, the only sound was the chattering of birds in the trees overhanging them. After a few minutes, Peter walked out of the Embassy door and approached the security kiosk.

"I'm Peter Bowen," he said to the guard, showing him the security tag hanging on a lanyard around his neck. "It's fine to let them through. They'll be with me."

"Yes, sir," the guard said. "Wear these, please." He handed Claire and Kristine each a lanyard with a "Visitor" tag hanging from it, and they followed Peter back into the building.

"What's up?" he asked as they walked.

"Kristine found something in my purse that we thought you'd be interested in."

"I'm intrigued," he said, smiling.

They entered the building. The lobby was a broad open area, with a marble floor and four tall marble columns reaching to the second floor. A metal detector doorway was off to the left, and a table holding small plastic bowls was beside a conveyor belt feeding into an x-ray scanner. Two armed Marines stood nearby.

Peter approached the guards. "They're with me," he said.

"Doesn't matter, sir," said the first Marine. "You will all still need to go through security." He pointed to plastic bins on the table. "Please completely empty your pockets and put the items in these bowls, put your purse on the conveyor belt, then step through one at a time."

Once through security, Peter led them to a conference room on the second floor. Dark cherry wood paneling covered three walls, and the fourth had floor to ceiling windows that looked out onto the tree lined Avenue Gabriel. Along one wall was a credenza holding a tray with two coffee carafes and a stack of paper cups. A long cherry wood conference table ran down the center of the room, and twelve rolling brown leather chairs were tucked up to it. Peter closed the door behind them, and motioned them to sit.

"So what's up?" he asked as he pulled out a chair and sat down. He raised his eyebrows expectantly.

Claire took the chip out of her purse and handed it to him. "Kristine found this in a side pocket of my purse. I never use that pocket, so I hadn't noticed it before." She sat back in her chair, watching his face, waiting to see what he had to say.

Peter turned the chip over in his hand, examining it, brows furrowed. "Hang on a second, I'll be right back," and he left the room.

Claire and Kristine sat silently, looking around the room. Their eyes met, and Kristine nervously smiled. After several minutes, Peter came back into the room, another man following right behind. He was in his fifties and had thick gray hair combed straight back. His brown suit fit snuggly over his broad shoulders. Claire thought he looked vaguely familiar, then realized that he was the older of the two men at the airport who had taken Suzie into custody.

"This is Special Agent Hart," Peter said. "He's with the CIA. This is Claire McKenna, and Kristine…?"

"Quintana."

"Peter showed me what you found and told me about being followed and attacked," Agent Hart began. "And you're right, this is what they've been after."

"What is it?" asked Claire.

"A data chip. We knew it was out there, and we were hoping to find it before the bad guys did."

"But what's on it? Why is it so important?" Claire asked with confusion.

Agent Hart looked at Peter, who gave a single nod of approval. "What I'm about to tell you doesn't leave this room," Agent Hart said. "Understood?"

Both of the women nodded.

Agent Hart leaned forward and folded his hands on the table. "Let me start at the beginning. Suzie Nichols worked as a data analyst at the CIA in Langley."

"She told me she worked as an administrative assistant for Health and Human Services," Claire said, confused.

"I'm not surprised that she lied. In any case, she came to our attention about six months ago, and we suspected that she had downloaded vital information about Islamic terrorist cells living under the radar in the United States and Europe. Names, addresses, that sort of thing. If the terrorists knew we had that kind of detailed information, it could cripple our surveillance of these sleeper cells. The terrorists could just change their names, move... basically go underground even deeper. We caught wind that she was offering to sell the chip for one million dollars to some top Islamic terrorists, and was going to meet them in Paris. Our mission was to intercept the chip and keep it out of the terrorists' hands."

"I remember seeing you and another man in the Customs area at the airport," Claire said.

Agent Hart nodded. "That's right. We detained Suzie and searched her and her carry-on bags, but found nothing. We figured she must have smuggled the chip in somehow, but didn't know how or where. As it turns out, she had planted the chip in your purse."

"How could she have done that?" Claire asked incredulously.

"Did you ever leave your purse while you were on the plane? Did you get up to go to the bathroom, or take a walk down the aisle?" Agent Hart asked.

Claire thought for a moment and slowly nodded.

"Well, there you go. She just slipped it into your bag when you were gone, and you were none the wiser. All she had to do then was to re-connect with you in Paris, and retrieve the chip."

"How did she know where I'd be? Paris is a huge city." Claire paused for a moment, then her face lit up with understanding. "Oh, wait a second," she said, "I did look at the paperwork for my apartment on the plane, and she even asked me about it. She could have seen the address then. And waited at the café near the apartment to 'accidentally' run into me. Damn!"

Agent Hart slowly nodded. "That would do it."

"You know," Claire continued, slowly nodding with comprehension, "now that I think about it, Suzie's demeanor did change on the plane. At first she seemed real preoccupied and distant, and just stared out the window. But then after a while, she warmed up and was real friendly."

"She had decided how she was going to get the chip through Customs," he said, "and needed to get close to you so she could get it back."

They were all silent for a moment. "The terrorists knew Suzie was going to be staying at the Grande Hôtel Sorbonne," Agent Hart said. "That first night, they went to the hotel to get the chip, but of course Suzie didn't have it. My guess is that she didn't tell them anything at first; maybe so she could still get the million dollars, or maybe just to protect you. But they tortured her, and she must have finally told them that you had it. They've been after you ever since, trying to retrieve it."

Claire thought for a moment. "Does Inspector Girard know about this?"

"Not yet, but we'll fill him in."

No one said anything for a minute. Agent Hart was silent as he studied Claire's face, then he spoke.

"So, Ms. McKenna, here's the deal…your country could use your help. As you know, terrorists are alive and well in the world, and they attacked several Parisian targets in 2015, including the simultaneous attacks in November that killed more than 130 people. We desperately want to capture the terrorist leadership in Paris, but we don't know who they are or where they're holed up." He paused. "We'd like you to help us."

"How?"

"The next time the terrorists contact you, and we know they will, you'll tell them you found the chip but you don't have it on you. You'll set up a meeting with them to hand it off. We'll give you a fake chip to give them, and we'll be watching. Once you've handed it off, you're done. You can just go on your way, and we'll follow the currier back to their leaders and arrest them."

Claire said nothing, her thoughts swirling, considering what had been asked of her. She folded her hands on the table and silently studied them, her thumbs slowly circling around each other. Kristine finally said what was going through Claire's head. "That sounds pretty dangerous," she said. "These people are ruthless. They could kill her."

"We'll be right there watching," said Agent Hart. "It will be perfectly safe for her."

Claire was silent for a moment. "And if I don't do it?" she softly asked.

"We'll get your passport back from the Paris police, and you can go home today." Agent Hart leaned forward in his chair, lacing his fingers together on the tabletop. His eyes locked with Claire's. "But be aware, if you choose not to help us, there is a high probability that there will be more terror attacks, and people will die, both here in France and at home."

"No pressure, huh?" said Kristine with sarcasm.

"How would I contact the terrorists? I don't know who they are, or where they're at."

"Peter said you moved out of your apartment this morning. To make it easier for the terrorists, we'd like you to move back in. Then, trust me, they'll find you," Agent Hart said. "And I promise, we'll be watching you to keep you safe." He leaned back in his chair, lacing his fingers together over his belly. "I assure you, nothing will happen to you."

Claire was quiet for a moment, and finally said, "Can I have a minute to think about this?"

"Of course," Agent Hart said. "I understand. It is a big decision. But don't take too long. The terrorists think you still have the chip, and they'll be coming after you again."

Claire met the agent's eyes with a steady stare. "Unless I go home today."

He nodded. "That's right. Unless you go home today."

Agent Hart stood up. "I'll leave you to think about what you want to do." He reached into his breast pocket and handed a business card to Claire. "If you need to talk to me, for whatever reason, you can call me at this number, day or night." She took the card and slid it into her pocket. He continued, "Peter, give me a shout when she decides."

Peter nodded, and the agent left the room.

"Jesus," Kristine said, shaking her head.

"No shit."

Peter said, "It's a tough decision, but an important one. It really could help us win the war against terrorism. Or at least one skirmish."

No one spoke for a moment, then Claire said, "Could we have a few minutes alone, please?"

"Of course." He got up and left the room.

The two women looked at each other in silence. After a moment, Kristine asked, "What do you think?"

Claire slowly shook her head. "I really don't know. I have mixed feelings. Part of me wants to help, but the other part feels like I've been through enough already. Like I just want to be safe, get the hell out of here, and go home."

"But on the other hand….corny as it may sound, your country needs you."

"I know." Claire was silent for a few moments, chewing her lower lip, thinking. "What would you do?"

"That's a tough question," Kristine said, leaning back in her chair. She thought for a few moments. "But I think I'd do it. Sometimes a person has to step up and do the right thing for the greater good."

Claire slowly shook her head, considering, unsure what to do. Neither woman spoke for quite some time. Claire absently traced circular patterns on the table-top with her finger. Finally, she nodded once with decision and said, "You're right. I'll do it."

CHAPTER EIGHT

Claire had to admit; it felt good to be back in her own apartment again. She and Kristine sat quietly on the balcony, sipping wine and lost in their own thoughts as they gazed down on the cobblestone street below. It was just after five o'clock, and people were heading home from work. Businessmen in crisply tailored suits, briefcases in hand, strolled by. Gaggles of students from the Sorbonne, backpacks slung over their shoulders, chatted and laughed as they swarmed over the sidewalk, their classes finished for the day. A middle aged woman wearing a skirt and jacket rode by on a bicycle, a baguette and bouquet of flowers tucked into the wicker basket on the front of her bike. Across the street a man in khaki slacks and a polo shirt sat at an outdoor café, reading the newspaper and sipping a glass of wine. He glanced up to their balcony and made eye contact with Claire, slowly nodded once, then resumed reading his paper.

"Looks like the surveillance boys are in place," Claire said, pointing across the street.

"I've got to hand it to you, Claire, you do make life interesting." Kristine flashed a grin.

Claire felt a sudden pang in her heart. She had really missed that impish grin. She missed everything about Kristine, if she were being honest with herself. She couldn't stop looking at her, thinking, reflecting on the past, and wondering about the future. Was there a future?

"What?" Kristine asked, cocking her head to one side.

"Nothing," said Claire. "Just thinking."

"That's dangerous." Again, that grin. "So, now what? We never did get lunch, and I'm starving."

Claire smiled; delighted to just be with the woman she loved. Loved? Did she actually use that word? "Well, they don't start serving dinner until 7:00."

"How about this?" she suggested, her face brightening. "I heard about these boat cruises that go down the Seine at night, from Notre Dame to the Eiffel Tower. It's supposed to be beautiful. What if we head down toward Notre Dame, grab a bite in a deli or someplace, and then take the cruise?"

*

It was just getting dark when they got to the tour boat near Notre Dame. It looked like a flat-bottomed, converted barge with a canopy covering rows of bench seats. A line of people waited on the dock to board. Many were senior citizens, the women in light summer dresses or slacks, the men in Dockers and white tennis shoes. Judging by the white tennis shoes, they were probably Americans. A young woman hostess greeted them and handed them headsets as they climbed on board.

"You can plug these in and select your language," the hostess said in very good English. "We will leave in just a few minutes."

Kristine and Claire found two seats near the side of the boat and sat down. They plugged in their headsets, and listened to snappy French Muzak while they waited for the boat to depart.

"This is great," said Kristine. "Having fun yet?"

114

Claire smiled and nodded. She was tempted, so tempted, to reach over and take Kristine's hand, but she knew she'd better not.

The cruise down the Seine truly was spectacular. They call Paris "the city of lights" for a reason, Claire thought. Historical buildings from the sixteenth century and more than a dozen bridges were all lit up, radiant in the night, and the taped commentary talked about the history of the city and each of the sights. When they finally reached the Eiffel Tower, it was covered with thousands of small lights, soaring like an illuminated dagger piercing the night sky. Suddenly, the tower burst into life, sparkling with brilliantly dancing lights, looking like glittering diamonds in the darkness. Everyone on the boat gasped, and "ooohs" and "ahhhs" pierced the still night.

"Oh, my God," said Kristine, slowly shaking her head in amazement. "I think I love Paris."

Claire smiled, and took Kristine's hand in the dark. "And I love you," she said softly.

Kristine met Claire's eyes, and they both smiled. She gave a little squeeze of Claire's hand and released it.

*

By the time the boat got back to Notre Dame, it was nearly ten o'clock. They walked back to the apartment in the warm Paris evening, the streets still crowded with people. Young lovers strolling hand in hand, older people stepping carefully, unsure of their footing, as they crossed the uneven, cobblestone streets. Claire and Kristine walked past closed shops and outdoor restaurants, light spilling out through open doors, late night diners sharing quiet conversations over their meals.

When they got to the apartment, Claire noticed a black sedan parked across the street with two men sitting in it. The CIA night shift, she thought.

She unlocked the apartment and turned on the lights. Kristine followed her, closing the door behind her. The two women looked at each other for a moment, neither speaking. Finally, Kristine smiled and softly said, "This has been a wonderful day."

Claire shrugged. "Aside from having been kidnapped and stabbed, I'd have to agree." She grinned.

"Sorry," she said contritely, "you're right." She gazed apologetically into Claire's eyes. "That was a horrible thing to say."

Claire slowly shook her head and smiled. "It's ok," she said, "I know what you meant."

Kristine stepped forward and gave Claire a warm hug. Claire could feel her breasts press softly against her chest. Kristine kissed her softly on the cheek, then released her and stepped back.

It's now or never, Claire thought. "We need to talk."

Kristine tipped her head with curiosity. "OK?" she said hesitantly.

Claire took her by the hand and led her to the couch. They sat side-by-side, thighs almost touching.

She briefly studied her hands in her lap, then met Kristine's steady gaze. "I've been thinking a lot about us, about what happened," she began hesitantly.

"Claire, don't…" Kristine shook her head.

"No, please, let me finish," she interrupted. "You were right. I was a jerk, and I should have spent more time with you."

Kristine searched Claire's face, confused, unsure of what was going on.

"All of this," she waved her hand to encompass the room, "all of what's been happening to me this past week…it's made me realize just how fragile life is, and what's really important in life. And what's important in my life is you, Kristine. You. Not work. Not being offered a partnership. It's you."

Neither woman said anything for a moment. Claire wondered if she had just put her foot in it, big time.

"I love you, Kristine," Claire said softly. Her eyes started to brim with tears. "I've always loved you, and I always will." She wiped a tear from her cheek. "I'm so sorry." She gave a wan smile.

Kristine looked thoughtfully at her for a moment and shook her head. "You big dope," she said with mock exasperation. She briefly grinned, then the smile faded, and she became serious. "I love you, too, honey. My life's been so empty without you these last few months." She took Claire's hand in her own and gave it a little squeeze. The two women looked into each other's eyes, plumbing the depths of their souls. Then Kristine broke the silence. "And you're right; you were a jerk." She grinned broadly.

Claire laughed.

"Let's go to bed," Kristine said.

"I only have the one bed," Claire said impishly.

"I know." Kristine smiled. She took Claire by the hand and led her to the bedroom.

*

Claire awakened early. Kristine lay on her side; facing Claire, still sound asleep, softly snoring. The covers were off her bare shoulders to her waist, and her voluptuous breasts lay full and inviting on the bed. Claire leaned over and gently kissed her breast. Kristine moaned, stirred and rolled onto her back, the weight of her breasts shifting toward her sides, then settled deeper into sleep. Claire smiled, truly happy for the first time in months.

She got up, showered, and put on some coffee. She poured herself a cup and sat on the couch, thinking about last night and how wonderful everything had turned out. Finally, it felt like her life was back on track, back where it should be. She picked up a tourist guide and began thumbing through it, wondering what they should do today.

"Is that coffee I smell?" Kristine said from the bedroom.

"Yes, ma'am. Would you like a cup?"

"You betcha."

Claire poured a cup of coffee and brought it in to her. Kristine propped both pillows under her head and sat up, smiling.

"Thanks," she said, taking the cup from Claire.

Claire leaned over and kissed her. Her lips were so soft, so full, so wonderful.

"I've got a great idea," Claire said. "When you finish your coffee, why don't you shower, and we'll go out for breakfast?"

*

They walked to a tiny café out on Rue Saint-Jacques. White lace curtains adorned the windows, and blue and white-checkered tablecloths were on the handful of small tables. They chose a table near the window and sat down. An older woman with an apron tied around her waist came over to them.

"*Bon jour*," the woman said as she handed each of them a menu. She was trim for her age and had gray hair pulled back in a French roll. Deep creases etched her forehead, and fine lines like parentheses bracketed her mouth.

"*Bon jour*," said Kristine. "*Deux café crème, s'il vous plaît.*"

The woman nodded and walked back to the counter.

Claire was stunned. "I didn't know you spoke French!" she exclaimed.

"I took three years in high school. It's rusty, but it's still in here somewhere," she said, tapping her forehead.

They scanned their menus.

"I have no idea what any of this is," Claire said. "Where's my French/English dictionary?" She started to dig through her purse.

The waitress came back to the table and set down two small cups of café au lait on saucers. Little paper tubes of sugar sat next to the cups, along with tiny spoons.

"Never mind, I'll take care of this," said Kristine. "*Nous voulons deux croissants avec confitures est deux verre de jus d'orange, s'il vous plaît.*"

The waitress nodded. "*Oui, madame*," and left.

"Wow, I'm impressed," said Claire, grinning.

Kristine laughed. "Well, don't be, at least not yet. We'll see if we actually get what I think I ordered. We could end up with pigs' feet and Brussels sprouts."

A few minutes later the waitress brought two croissants, jam, and two glasses of orange juice.

"What," Claire said, "no omelets? No hash browns?"

"The French don't usually eat omelets for breakfast. This," she waved her hand over the food in front of them, "is a typical French breakfast. *Bon apétit!*"

It was going to be a good morning, Claire thought. Felt like old times. They ate their breakfast, chatting and laughing about nothing in particular, just enjoying each other's company.

"So what do you want to do today? What do you want to see?" Claire asked as she nibbled her croissant.

"The Louvre would be nice…or Notre Dame?"

"Too many bad memories of being chased."

"Sacré-Coeur?"

"Really? You want me to return to the scene of the crime?"

Kristine thought for a moment and burst out, "Ooo! Ooo! I know! Let's go back to the Champs Elysées and do some shopping! I could use a new Gucci handbag and some Louis Vuitton clothes!"

Claire threw back her head and laughed. God, it felt good to laugh again! "Are you kidding me? The closest you've ever been to 'Gucci' is going to Mama Gucci's Italian restaurant in D.C.!" She grinned at Kristine.

"C'mon," Kristine pleaded, tipping her head and begging with her eyes, "It'll be fun to hang around with all those rich and famous people."

"And a million other tourists gawking and taking pictures."

Claire grinned, then glanced past Kristine toward the door. A tall, thin, older Middle Eastern man, dressed in a long white robe with a light blue, embroidered *kufi* skullcap, came into the restaurant and scanned the room. When he spotted Claire he started to walk toward them.

Her smile faded. "Oh, oh," Claire said softly.

"What?"

The man approached their table, glanced at Kristine, and pulled up a chair.

"Hello, Madame McKenna."

Claire said nothing. Where were her CIA shadows?

"I think you know why I am here." His gaze bore into her eyes. "We want that data chip. My colleagues have not been very…" he paused, searching for the word, "subtle, and I apologize for that. I thought that perhaps, another approach, a more civilized approach, might be more successful. We mean you no harm."

"Really?" Claire asked incredulously. "Is that why I have twenty six stitches in my side? And what about Suzie? Did you mean her no harm, either?"

"That was unfortunate. We want to be reasonable. We want that chip, and we will get it." He paused for a moment, adding meaningfully, "One way or another."

Claire eyed him with barely veiled hostility. "I don't have it on me."

The man nodded. "No, of course not. But you do have it, correct?"

"Yes."

"Good. Bring the chip to the plaza in front of the Pantheon at 9:00 tonight. I will meet you, and then we can all go on with our lives."

"No," said Claire, shaking her head. "I don't think so. No one would be around at that time of night. It's too isolated, and I don't trust you." She met his gaze with a steady stare, confident, secure, and full of a bravado that she didn't feel. "Here's what's going to happen."

The man smiled at Claire with genuine respect.

"We'll meet in two hours on Boulevard Saint-Michel, near Rue des Écoles, in front of the Starbucks."

The man grinned. "I like you," he said, "even if you are a woman. You have courage. It is unfortunate that we are adversaries." He grew serious. "All right, as you wish.

My friend will be there in two hours. But do not go to the police, or I assure you, you will be sorry. And please give me your cell phone number."

Claire rattled off her phone number. The man punched it into his phone, then stood and headed for the entrance.

"Hey!" Claire called after him. He stopped and turned to face her. "You know my name; what's yours?"

The man briefly smiled. "Samir," he said, then proceeded to the door and left.

Claire blew out a long breath of relief and slid down in her chair, stretching her legs out in front of her. She looked at Kristine, and raised her eyebrows.

"Jesus," Kristine said with amazement, "you've got more guts than a sausage factory."

Claire smiled and shrugged. "Well…sometimes strength is good. 'The best defense being a good offense' and all that." She glanced out the window. "Here he comes."

Kristine reached into her pocket and quickly pulled out her phone. As the man walked past their window, she snapped a picture of him. "Just in case," she said.

*

They walked back to the apartment, each woman deep in her own thoughts. As soon as they got home, Claire called Agent Hart and told him about the scheduled meeting.

"They didn't waste any time."

"Where were your agents?" Claire asked. "I didn't see anybody when we were in the restaurant."

"They were there, but they didn't want to tip their hand yet. But trust me, we'll have agents deployed around the Starbucks when you make the hand off, and I'll let Inspector Girard know what's going on to keep him in the loop. Once you've given them the chip, we'll follow the person back to their home base. You could be back home in D.C. by this evening."

"I can't wait."

"I'll have one of our agents bring you the fake chip within the next thirty minutes."

"Kristine got a picture of the man who met with us," Claire said. "His name is Samir."

"Could you send it to me? We can run it through our facial recognition software and see if we come up with anything. And again, thanks for your help."

*

Two hours later, Claire walked down Boulevard Saint-Michel toward the Seine, the sun warm on her face, fluffy white clouds drifting through a deep blue sky. She had told Kristine she thought it would be best if she waited in the apartment until after the exchange was over. Kristine wasn't happy about it, but finally agreed.

She was nervous about meeting the man and handing off the data chip, but at the same time she couldn't wait to put all of this behind her, go home to D.C. with Kristine, and try to rebuild their lives. She put her hand in her pocket and fingered the chip. Agent Hart had told her it wasn't a blank chip, but rather had outdated data on it. He told her not to worry, the terrorists would never know because they'd arrest them as soon as they got back to their main base, before they even had a chance to examine the chip. She hoped he was right.

She passed an older, tattered man hobbling along the sidewalk with crutches, half dragging one deformed foot behind him. It occurred to her that she had seen lots of people with what looked like congenital deformities on the streets of Paris, many more than she would have seen at home. Inadequate health care when they were young? No money for treatment? Immigrants from third world countries? She didn't know, but it saddened her because she bet many of them could have been helped if they had grown up in the States.

She glanced up toward the tops of the buildings and looked around. Paris really was a beautiful city. The stone art work in the architecture, gargoyles glaring at passersby, bright red geraniums trailing over the black wrought iron railings of the balconies on so many of the buildings. Once this was all over, she would love to come back with Kristine and spend some time here, just the two of them, and enjoy the city.

She arrived at the Starbucks and stopped in the middle of the sidewalk, looking around, pedestrians parting like the Red Sea and flowing around her. She spotted an empty table, sat, and waited. She glanced at her watch; right on time.

A few moments later she saw a young Middle Eastern man walk toward her in his long white robe and red *kufi*. She could feel her heart begin to pound in her chest. He was perhaps fifteen feet away when suddenly the sound of approaching sirens pierced the air. Claire looked up the street and saw two Paris police cars, red and blue lights flashing, race down Boulevard Saint-Michel coming right at them. She shot a glance back at the man, who met her eyes with a piercing stare. Claire raised her shoulders and her hands, palms up, in an "I have no idea" shrug and shook her head. The police cars drew nearer. The man turned and ran down a side street. The police cars approached the Starbucks and drove past, then turned down a street going the opposite direction than the man had taken.

"God damn it!" she blurted out, stamping her foot with frustration. A young woman passing by shot her a curious glance and kept walking.

She called Agent Hart as soon as she got back to the apartment, and he came over within half an hour. Kristine had made a pot of coffee, and they all sat in the living room.

"We had nothing to do with that," he said. "It was just a horrible coincidence, really bad timing." Agent Hart sadly shook his head. "Inspector Girard should have made sure something like this didn't happen. But it did." He took a sip of his coffee and set the cup down on the coffee table.

"They'll think *I* called the cops," Claire exclaimed in frustration. "Now what?"

Kristine shook her head in disbelief. "I think we should just go home."

They were all silent for a moment.

"Well," began Agent Hart, "certainly no one would blame you if you did leave." He took another sip of coffee, giving a moment for his comment to sink in. "Or, we could try one more time. We really need to get these guys. And I'm sure they'll contact you again." He picked up a pastry that Kristine had put out on the table and bit into it, crumbs cascading to his lap. He brushed them onto his napkin and set it on the table. He looked from Claire to Kristine, then back to Claire again.

Long silent moments passed. Kristine stared at Claire, pleading with her eyes. She could feel her gaze bore into her, but couldn't bring herself to look back.

Finally, Claire said, "Okay," with resignation. "One more try, then we're out of here."

Kristine sighed heavily with frustration and leaned back in her chair, shaking her head in disgust.

Agent Hart stood to leave. "Let me know when they reach out to you. And in the meantime, my agents will still be keeping you under surveillance."

The two women were finally alone in the living room.

"You're a lot nicer than I would be, that's for damned sure," Kristine said bitterly.

"Well....it seems like the right thing to do." Claire gave a meek smile. "It'll be over soon, I promise."

"That's not a promise you can keep," she said angrily. She stood and went into the bedroom.

Claire sat back on the couch and shook her head. Crap. What do I do? Keep Kristine happy? Or try to help my country? After a few minutes of mental struggle, she decided she needed some air to try and clear her mind.

"I'm going for a walk," she said. No reply. Claire grabbed her key, and left.

*

She slowly walked down Rue Cujas, trying to mentally sort things out. It seemed like a no-win situation, but in her heart she knew she had made the right decision.

She stepped out onto the street and glanced left and right. No sign of any CIA men, but she assumed they were there somewhere, watching. She walked up toward the Pantheon, deep in thought. She strolled past a homeless man asleep under a cardboard shelter, the walls and ceiling tied together with pieces of string. As she went by, she heard someone behind her and turned.

"You should not have called the police." Samir glared at her with a combination of contempt and disappointment.

"I didn't," Claire exclaimed. "Those police cars were just a coincidence, honest!"

The man considered her for a moment, neither one saying anything, eyes locked on each other. Finally, he said, "All right. One more chance. Have you been to the Eiffel Tower? It is a wonderful thing, so beautiful. You will bring the chip to the plaza beneath the Eiffel Tower in two hours. You will meet a woman there, near the southern leg of the tower, and you will give her the chip. If you do not, well…… I will not be responsible for what my colleagues do next."

"All right. I'll be there. What does the woman look like?"

"She will find you. And come alone," he said. "No police, or I assure you, it will be very unpleasant for you and your friend."

"I understand."

Samir turned and left. Claire called after him, "You know, all of this isn't exactly my idea of fun, either!" He waved dismissively over his shoulder and kept walking.

She headed back to the apartment and called Agent Hart.

"My men saw what happened. The terrorists are really desperate to get that chip," he said.

Claire and Kristine sat side by side on the couch in their living room. Claire shifted the phone to her other ear so Kristine could hear, too.

"We'll have agents deployed around the plaza," he told her. "And I'll call Inspector Girard. Once you've made the hand off, we'll follow the woman back to their home base. You'll be free to leave as soon as you like after that."

*

The Eiffel Tower soared over a broad plaza area filled with tourists and vendors selling laser penlights, Eiffel Tower key chains and other trinkets. A long line of tourists waited to go up the elevator within the tower, while another line was in front of a concession stand to buy ice cream, soft drinks and coffee.

Claire stood near the southern leg of the tower and glanced around. Who were the CIA agents? The woman over there at the concession stand, looking at post cards? The young man in spandex bike shorts fiddling with his bicycle? She couldn't tell, and hopefully the woman who was coming to meet her wouldn't be able to tell, either.

She glanced up at the tower soaring above her, a latticework of iron girders crisscrossing in each of the four splayed legs, tall metal archways spanning between adjacent buttresses. What a spectacular piece of engineering, she thought, considering it was built in the 1880s. She wished that she had time to take the elevator to the top of the tower for the view of Paris. Oh, well, she thought; maybe someday.

She walked over to a bench and sat down, glancing around. Soon, she thought. Soon this will all be over.

A cluster of perhaps ten women in black burqas entered the plaza and looked around. The burqas completely covered their bodies, with a dark mesh screen covering their eyes. After a moment, one of the burqa-clad women broke away from the group and walked over to Claire.

"Do you 'ave eet?" It was a woman's voice, with a pronounced French accent.

"Yes." She pulled the chip out of her pocket and handed it to the woman.

"*Merci*." She turned and walked back to the group of women in burqas and was immediately engulfed by them, their arms reaching toward each other, making it impossible to tell who was who, or who had the chip. Then the group scattered, each one heading in a different direction, ten different targets for the CIA to follow.

"Shit!" Claire exclaimed, running her fingers through her hair in frustration. She saw a few of the people who had been in the plaza start to follow several of the women, but then hesitate, and stop. Who had the chip?

Claire shook her head in frustration. That's it, she thought, I've had enough. I just want to go home.

*

When she got back to the apartment, she told Kristine what had happened.

"You're kidding! They were in burqas?" Kristine shook her head in disbelief. "What now?"

"Wait to hear from Agent Hart, I guess. I'll ask him for my passport, then let's go home."

Kristine poured a glass of wine for each of them, and they sat out on the balcony in silence, each in her own thoughts, waiting for the agent's call. The phone soon rang.

"Well, we lost them," he began. "But it was worth the try. You're free to fly home, with our thanks. We've taken the liberty of booking you with two first class tickets on

Avion Air flight 357 to D.C., leaving Charles de Gaulle airport tomorrow morning at 11:10. The tickets will be waiting for you at the Avion Air counter. And the CIA paid for your tickets, out of gratitude."

"When can I get my passport?"

"I'll call Inspector Girard, and have someone bring it to the apartment this afternoon. I'm sorry it turned out this way, but your country does appreciate your efforts in trying to help."

Claire hung up the phone and looked at Kristine. "Well, it's over. We've got a flight out tomorrow morning. First class, even."

"Nice." She thought for a moment. "So we've got the afternoon to enjoy Paris. What shall we do?"

"You decide."

Kristine gazed toward the ceiling, pretending to think, finger tapping her lips. "Hmmmmmm…" She smiled a coquettish grin. "The Champs Elysées? Shopping?"

Claire rolled her eyes in mock annoyance. "Oh, all right, whatever." Then she chuckled. "Let me take a look at the Metro map."

*

They took the RER B Metro to Châtelet Les Halles, and then switched to the #1 line heading toward La Défense. They got off at the Concorde station, climbed the stairs to street level, and looked around. A tall obelisk made of yellow granite and covered in Egyptian hieroglyphics soared right in front of them, while the Avenue des Champs Elysées ran out to the west. In the distance at the far end of the Avenue des Champs Elysées rose the Arc de Triomphe.

"Why do I have a sense of *deva vu*?" asked Kristine.

130

"The American Embassy is right over there," Claire replied, pointing to the north.

They meandered down the Champs Elysées, past a Porsche dealership with snazzy sports cars on display inside the storefront. They window shopped at Cartier, astonished by the prices of its luxurious jewelry, then walked past Armani, Chanel, Christian Dior…

"Geez, Kristine, if you keep drooling like that I'm going to have to get you a bib."

Kristine laughed. "Doesn't cost anything to look, right?"

They had a bite to eat at an outdoor café, shared a bottle of wine, and by the time they got back to the apartment that evening they were both exhausted but happy.

"What a great day," Kristine said.

Claire nodded. "We'd better hit the sack. We should leave the apartment by 8:15 if we're going to get that flight."

*

They went to bed. Both of them were too tired to do anything but sleep, and Claire was happy just to lie naked next to the woman she loved and feel the warmth of her body alongside her.

Morning came much too soon. Claire got in the shower first, got dressed, and went out to the kitchen to put on the coffee. Kristine showered, and as she was getting dressed she called out, "What time did you say that we'll need to leave the apartment for the airport?"

"Eight fifteen."

Kristine came into the kitchen. "You know, I still haven't seen all that much of Paris. I know you're going to have to pack, but would you mind if I took a walk and just looked around a little?"

"Not at all. Do you want my compass so you don't get lost?"

Kristine gave her a 'do you think I'm an idiot' look. "I don't need no stinking compass," she said sarcastically. She tapped her forehead. "It's all right here. I'll be just fine."

"OK, but be sure you're back by 8:15."

CHAPTER NINE

Kristine stepped out onto Rue Cujas and glanced around. The street was empty, no people and no cars except for a badly dented, old sage green Peugeot parked across the street. She could just barely see the dome of the Pantheon peeking over other buildings to her left. She thought, why not, and started walking in that direction.

The morning was cool and overcast, dark clouds scuttling overhead. It smelled like rain was on the way, maybe even a thunderstorm. Quite a change from the heat of the past two days. Kristine strolled past a *boulangerie*, the decadent pastries in the window seducing her, begging her to come in and sample some. After eyeing the delectables for a few minutes and struggling with the decision, she gave in to temptation and entered the bakery. After all, when would she be in Paris again? And what's a few hundred calories? Per bite, she admitted to herself.

"*Bon jour*," she smiled and said to the clerk as she entered.

"*Bon jour, madame.*" The clerk was in the midst of helping an elderly man with his purchase. He was dressed in a light blue sport coat and cream-colored slacks, his gray hair peeking out from beneath his white cotton cap. She took the coins that he handed her, then gave him a small, flat, white paper sack containing his pastries.

"*Merci, monsieur. Au revoir.*"

133

"*Au revoir, Madame,*" the man replied, touched the brim of his cap, and walked out the door.

The clerk turned to Kristine and said, "*Ce que vous voulez, madame?*"

Kristine scanned the glass case with its pastries on display. What do I want, what do I want…So hard to decide. "*C'est très difficile.*" Finally, she pointed to a chocolate éclair. "*Je voudrais que l'éclair, s'il vous plaît.*

The clerk picked up a square of waxed paper, selected an éclair and slipped it into a sack.

"*Deux euro,*" she said.

Kristine handed the woman a two Euro coin and took the sack.

"*Merci, au revoir,*" said the clerk.

"*Au revoir, madame,*" replied Kristine. She slid the pastry from its bag and took a bite before she even left the shop. Oh, my god, that's good.

Kristine slowly walked down the street, slowly nibbling at the pastry just to make it last longer. She passed a store selling eyeglasses and a *tabac* store, both closed at this time of the morning. She took the last bite of her pastry and tossed the paper sleeve into a garbage bin, and kept walking down the street. The Pantheon loomed ahead.

The street was quiet, incredibly peaceful for a big city. The only sounds she could hear were birds chirping in the branches of the trees high above her head. A vehicle driving up behind her soon broke the early morning silence. She heard a car door open, then running footsteps. She started to turn to see what was going on, but before she could look she felt a sharp blow on the back of her head. Stars flickered before her eyes before everything went black.

My god, what a headache, Kristine thought. She slowly opened her eyes. A small, olive skinned boy dressed in a white robe, a light blue *kufi* perched on his curly black hair, stood directly in front of her, intently peering into her face. His huge brown eyes were like molten chocolate, making him look like one of those big-eyed kids in a Margaret Keane painting. When Kristine's gaze met his, his eyes grew even wider with fear.

"Papa!" he shouted and ran from the room.

Kristine was tied to a chair, both of her arms secured to the arms of the chair. Her head throbbed with pain, and she was a little nauseated. Concussion? She had no idea.

She looked around. She was in a bedroom, and a pair of hot pink shoes was on the floor near the bed. She had been wearing a pair just like that. She glanced down at her feet and saw that she was in her stocking feet. Why would they have taken her shoes off? Then she realized that maybe it was to make her less likely to run away. As if she could.

The double bed was covered with a deep purple bedspread, and gold silk pillows adorned the head of the bed. The walls were covered with gold and red wallpaper with a distinct Arab design, and heavy red draperies were pulled back from the French windows. A small desk sat along one wall, and apparently it was that desk chair that Kristine was now tied to.

A moment later Samir came into the room, the small boy following in his wake. The man smiled, but without warmth.

"Hello again," he began. "I am sorry this had to happen, but I did warn you and your friend not to play with us or get the police involved." He shook his head sadly.

"Your friend gave us a useless chip, not the one Suzie had given her. Ms. McKenna must have gone to the police or to your embassy, and they have tried to trap us." He looked steadily at Kristine. "It is unfortunate, but now we must do things we really did not want to do."

Kristine's thoughts were racing. How did she want to play this?

"I don't know anything about this," she said, "and I haven't done anything to you."

He slowly shook his head again, as if dealing with a dim-witted child. "But you will be the one to pay the price." He looked at Kristine's left hand and gently raised it up, her forearm still tightly secured to the arm of the chair. He fingered her pinky ring; the one Claire had given her all those years before. He gently ran his thumb over the ring.

"This ring…it is important to you and your friend? She would recognize it?"

Kristine was silent, watching his eyes, trying to read what he was thinking, trying to tell what was about to happen. Icy fear gripped her belly. Her heart raced, and her breath came in short little gasps.

"Hakim!" he called out over his shoulder. A few minutes later, another man entered the room. He was middle aged, shorter and heavier than Samir, with a moustache and scruffy five o'clock shadow. His eyes peered out from beneath heavy lids. He wore white linen pants and a pull over linen shirt, open at the throat. He carried a set of pruning shears in one hand. Samir said something to Hakim in Arabic, pointing at the pruning shears. Hakim responded with what seemed to be annoyance, shaking the pruning shears at Samir, and then pointing at Kristine's hand.

Kristine broke out in a cold sweat of panic.

136

Samir shook his head, also pointing at Kristine's hand, and responded in Arabic, his voice rising with anger. Samir lifted Kristine's little finger with one hand, pointed at the pruning shears, and spewed out more Arabic with fury.

Kristine frantically tried to free her hand from Samir's grip, terrified of what she was certain was about to happen, but her arm remained secured to the chair.

"Please, don't," she whimpered. "I haven't done anything to you."

Samir scowled at Hakim, then turned to Kristine. "Perhaps if we send your friend something to show that we are serious, she will stop toying with us and give us what we want," he said with irritation.

Tears started streaming down Kristine's face. "Oh, god no, please don't, please don't!"

"Hakim?" Samir said, and followed it with something in Arabic.

"NO!!!"

CHAPTER TEN

Claire glanced at her watch. Eight oh five. They needed to leave for the airport in ten minutes. Where the hell is Kristine, she thought. Damn it, I don't want to miss that flight! I bet she got lost. These streets are tricky, they curve and their names can change block by block. Damn it, I knew she should have taken that goddamn compass!

She nervously paced back and forth in the apartment. Their suitcases stood right next to the door, her purse on top, ready to go. Thunder rumbled in the distance, and she could hear buckets of rain start a relentless drumming on the balcony.

Claire heard a sound at the door, and a gentle tap.

"Finally," she muttered bitterly to herself and opened the door.

No one was there. She furrowed her brow, confused, and then noticed a small box on the door step. She picked it up and went back into the apartment, closing the door behind her, and sat on the couch.

It was a jewelry box with a red velvet lid and base, and a hinge on one side. She opened the box. Inside was a gold ring. She picked it up and recognized it at once; it was Kristine's. Confused, she leaned back on the couch, turning the ring over and over between her fingers. She looked back into the box and noticed a small piece of folded paper. She pulled it out and unfolded it.

"You gave us a worthless chip. We warned you not to go to the police, yet you did," the note read. "You and your government must pay for your betrayal. If you want your friend back alive, you must give us ten million American dollars in ransom. You have seventy-two hours; if you do not give us the money, the next box will contain your friend's head. Call us to arrange the exchange." A Paris phone number was then listed.

Claire leaned back on the couch, stunned. She ran her fingers through her hair, and slowly shook her head. Fuck. Fuck. Fuck. What does she do now?

She went over to the luggage and grabbed her purse, rummaged through, and pulled out Peter's card. She picked up her phone and dialed. He answered on the second ring.

"Hello, this is Peter Bowen, how can I help you?"

"Peter, it's Claire. I need your help."

"What's up?"

"They have Kristine."

"What do you mean, 'they have Kristine?'"

"They have her!" she shouted into the phone, all of her pent up emotion suddenly spewing out in a venomous outburst. "They took her! And they sent me her ring with a threat to kill her unless we give them ten million dollars in ransom!" Her chest heaved with fury, tears of frustration filling her eyes.

Peter was silent for a moment before he said, "We've got to tell Agent Hart. How soon can you be at the Embassy?"

*

They sat in the same conference room where they had met before. Agent Hart and Peter exchanged a knowing look, and then they both looked somberly at Claire.

"I can't begin to tell you how sorry I am that this has happened," Agent Hart began. "We should have kept you under surveillance until you actually got on that plane."

"You think?" she said sarcastically.

"Frankly, I'm surprised that they only sent you the ring. The terrorists that I've dealt with in the past were brutal, ruthless men, and they would have sent you the whole finger. That may be a good sign that they really don't want to hurt your friend."

No one said anything for a moment.

"So what do we do now? What's the plan?" She looked expectantly from one man to the other.

Agent Hart studied his folded hands on the table. "I'm terribly sorry, but I'm afraid there's nothing we can do to help with the ransom."

"What are you talking about?" Claire burst out with astonishment. She glared at Agent Hart in disbelief, then shot Peter a glance. He quickly avoided her eyes, staring off into space over her shoulder.

"The State Department's policy is that we don't negotiate with terrorists." The agent sadly shook his head. "I'm sorry, but we're unable to help. We can't intervene. We will try to discover where she's being held and, if feasible, try a rescue, but financially, I'm afraid you're on your own."

She glared at Agent Hart, seething with anger. "So let me get this straight," she said, her voice steady and cool, but with an undercurrent of unmistakable rage. "You asked me to risk my life to help you out with this data chip *bullshit*, and then when things head south, you wash your hands of the whole thing and say that nothing can be done? You'd let an innocent American citizen be brutally murdered, and you'd just sit back and let it happen?"

The room was deadly quiet. The two men stared at the table in an awkward silence. Agent Hart slowly shook his head. Peter nervously fiddled with his thumbs, absently picking at a hangnail. The clock ticked on the wall, the only sound in the hushed room.

"I'm really sorry, Claire," Peter said softly.

"Fuck you." Claire spat with disgust as she got to her feet. "Fuck all of you." She stalked out of the room.

The two men silently looked at each other. Agent Hart raised his eyebrows and shrugged helplessly.

"Really?" Peter asked. "There's nothing we can do? It does seem unfair."

Agent Hart sadly shook his head. "You know the rules."

*

Claire's head was swimming as she made her way back to her apartment. What the hell does she do now? Who can help her?

By the time she got back to her apartment, the rain had stopped, but the thunder still rumbled in the distance. It wasn't even noon yet, but she poured herself a glass of wine and went out to the balcony. She sat looking out across the Paris skyline, lost in her thoughts, unsure what to do. What *could* she do? After several minutes, she pulled out her phone.

"*Allô?*"

"Samir? This is Claire."

The line was briefly silent. "Do you have the money?" he asked.

"No. The Embassy says that the United States doesn't negotiate with terrorists, and they won't pay the money. And I certainly don't have ten million dollars."

Samir was silent for a moment and said, "That is unfortunate."

"I have some savings, and an IRA and 401K account. I can probably come up with $180,000. It's the best I can do. But it will take some time."

"It is not enough."

Claire's anger rose to the surface again. "Why do you want to hurt me? To hurt us? This isn't about politics or governments anymore; it's about real human beings who haven't done anything to hurt you or any of your loved ones. People who are only trying to get on with their own lives the best they can." She paused for a second, trying to regain control of her emotions. "Would Allah approve of this? Come on!"

The line was silent for a moment. "You are a *kafir*, an infidel. Allah would understand."

Claire was fuming with frustration and anger. "How do I even know that Kristine is still alive? I want to talk to her."

The line was again silent. Claire could hear movement of someone walking, and then faintly heard Samir say, "Speak."

"Hello?" Kristine timidly said.

"Kristine, are you ok?"

"Claire?"

Samir took the phone back. "You see, she is still alive. If you want to keep her that way, get the money."

He hung up. Kristine met his eyes. "What is it that you want?"

"Ransom, to punish the infidels for trying to deceive us."

"How much?"

Samir waved his hand dismissively. "An insignificant amount. All of you Americans are rich."

Kristine laughed derisively. "Are you kidding me? Claire's financially barely able to keep her head above water! She has a huge car payment, plus rent, and she's still paying off her student loans!"

"At least she can afford a car and a place to live, and has an education. That is more than most other people in the world. More than my family had in Iraq."

The little boy who had first met Kristine sneaked back into the room and stood behind his father, peeking around his legs. Kristine met his gaze. She may have a huge issue with his father, but this little guy had nothing to do with it. She smiled. The little boy meekly smiled back.

"What's your name?"

"His name is Jabar."

Kristine's arms were still tied to the arms of the chair, but she wiggled her fingers in a wave at the little boy. He shyly ducked his head behind his father.

"He's awfully sweet," Kristine said.

A brief smile of paternal pride flicked across Samir's face, then he turned and left, Jabar following in his wake. At the door, the boy turned and smiled again, then wiggled his fingers in a wave back at Kristine. Kristine grinned, and the boy left.

Kristine gazed around the room, and heaved a sigh. Now what? She tested the ropes, but they held her securely to the chair. She sighed again. *Claire will get me out of this. She won't let me down. She never has.*

*

Inspector Girard sat in Agent Hart's office. The Inspector's legs were crossed at the ankle and stretched out in front of him, hands folded and resting comfortably in his lap, giving an appearance of casualness that he certainly didn't feel. He gazed around the room. A picture of President Obama gazed out at him from the wall behind the desk. Several award plaques hung on either side of the photo. Papers were piled high on the desk, and a stained coffee mug was perched on top of a stack of files. Inspector Girard hated clutter, but apparently it didn't bother the American agent.

Agent Hart sat with his hands on the desk, fingers laced together, and peered at the Inspector. "We took the picture that Kristine had taken of the older man and ran it through our facial recognition software and got a hit," he said. "Samir Akbar. He lives on Rue Coypel, near Place d'Italie, in an apartment. Have you come across this name before?"

Inspector Girard shook his head. "No, it does not seem familiar."

"We've suspected that he's been involved with an Islamic terrorist cell in Paris for quite a while, and this pretty much confirms it." Agent Hart leaned back in his chair. "At this point, we don't have enough to go on to have you make an arrest."

Inspector Girard's teeth clenched imperceptibly. *Arrogant American CIA*, he thought. *They think they are so supérieur, so hautain...what is the English word? Haughty.*

Yes, haughty. They act like this is their country, and they are in charge. Like they decide what happens in Paris, and I am just their servant, their obedient "poodle", and must obey their orders.

"With all due respect," Inspector Girard said evenly, "I will be the one to decide when I have enough for an arrest."

Agent Hart locked eyes with Inspector Girard. No one had openly challenged Agent Hart since he first became an agent with the CIA thirty years ago. If he were in the States, he would never have tolerated such insubordinate behavior. And regardless of what Inspector Girard probably thought, Agent Hart did consider him to be his subordinate. After all, he was a senior Special Agent with the CIA. Fucking French cops.

Neither man said anything, the tension in the room palpable for a few minutes. Finally, Agent Hart said, "Of course. With your permission, we would like to post an agent across the street from Akbar's apartment to do surveillance, just in case that's where Ms. Quintana is being held. The agent can use a heat detecting device to see how many people are in the apartment and if it looks like she's there."

"That would be fine," Inspector Girard said. "My men will coordinate with your agents, and we will put ground surveillance in place." Inspector Girard got up to leave. "The important thing to remember," he said, "is that we want Ms. Quintana to be found safe. If we capture the terrorists, it will be…as you Americans say, 'icing on the éclair'. "

"My men will be in place by 1900 hours this evening."

CHAPTER ELEVEN

Kristine had been sitting in the chair for a long time, trying to sort out what to do. Not a lot of options, she thought. After a while her legs and arms started to ache from not moving. She repeatedly tightened and relaxed her arm and leg muscles trying to increase blood flow and relieve the cramps, but it didn't help a whole lot.

She must have dozed off, and awoke to the sound of movement outside the door. Hakim came into the room carrying a tray of food. Balancing her dinner on one hand, with the other he pulled a small table over and placed it in front of Kristine, then set her tray down. He untied her hands and pulled up a chair across from her and sat, eyes intent on what she was doing. Kristine rubbed her wrists to get the circulation going after the tight binds. She had no idea what was on the plate, but it did smell good.

Kristine glanced at her watch; just after 6:00. Despite all of the stress and excitement, she was starving, and couldn't wait to eat something. Steamed rice in some kind of a sauce…maybe yogurt? With some kind of light meat, perhaps lamb or chicken. She wasn't sure. She thought she could smell coriander and maybe cardamom.

She remembered hearing that it was a good idea for hostages to try to become "human" to their captors, to seem like real people and not just the enemy. Worth a shot, she figured. "*Parlez vous Anglais*?" she asked Hakim. He remained silent, staring at her.

"*Parlez vous français*?" Again, no response. No scintillating dinner companion tonight, she thought. Oh, well.

She took a forkful. My god, this stuff was good.

The little boy came into the room and stood next to Hakim. Kristine smiled. "How old are you, Jabar?"

The boy just blankly looked at her.

Where is my high school French when I need it? After a moment of thinking, she said, "*Quel âge as-tu*?"

The boy held up 4 fingers.

"Four! Very good!" She thought for a second and said, "*Quatre! Très bien*!" She smiled. Jabar smiled back.

She picked up her spoon, steamed it with her breath, and then hung the spoon from her nose. She made a goofy face. Jabar burst out in gales of laughter, doubling over and holding his sides, and Kristine laughed, too. Even Hakim smiled. Success, she thought.

She finished eating and wanted to lick the plate, but thought that might be too tacky. Hakim cleared the dishes and left, the boy trailing behind. As he went out the door, Jabar turned and waved, grinning. Kristine waved back. Cute kid, she thought.

*

Kristine was alone in the room, and felt an itch on her foot and scratched it. It suddenly dawned on her… Hakim must have been so preoccupied with clearing the dinner dishes that he forgot to tie her hands again. She untied the ropes at her ankles, stood up and started to explore. She walked to the French windows opening onto a small balcony and looked out. She noticed that the balcony butted up against an adjacent balcony. She tried the latch on the windows; locked. She looked down at the street below. They must be on a second or third floor apartment; too far to jump. Pedestrians strolled by, oblivious to the captive situation above them.

She walked over to the desk and started going through drawers. She found a letter opener and slipped it in her pocket. Never know when that might come in handy.

I can't just sit here and wait to see what they have planned for me, she thought. Claire's never going to be able to get a big ransom together, and I know the U.S. won't negotiate with terrorists. She looked around the room again. She walked over to the bed, picked up the nightstand, and carried it over to the French windows. Here goes nothing, she thought.

She swung the table into the French window, glass shattering, showering shards over the balcony and onto the ground below.

"Help!" she screamed as she climbed through the broken window and onto the balcony. "Help!"

People on the ground looked up with curiosity. Still screaming for help, Kristine climbed over her balcony railing and onto the adjacent balcony. Several people on the street pulled out their cell phones and dialed.

It was a warm July evening and the French windows were open on the other balcony. Kristine pushed curtains aside and stepped over the windowsill. A woman in a floral gown and scarf looked up, surprised. A moment later, Samir entered the room and rushed toward Kristine. Shit. It was the same apartment, just a different balcony.

Kristine turned and dove for the window, still screaming "Help". She tried to get back onto the balcony, but Samir grabbed her, clapped his hand over her mouth, and with his other arm around her chest, pulled her back inside. He dragged her toward the door as the gowned woman passively watched.

Kristine managed to get her hand into her pocket and pulled out the letter opener, then thrust it as hard as she could over her shoulder, stabbing it deeply into Samir's arm. He shrieked in pain and released Kristine as he grabbed for his bleeding arm. Kristine ran, ran as fast as she could out of the room. She tore into the living room, and ploughed straight into Hakim, bouncing back several steps after the impact. They both looked at each other for a second with surprise, then Hakim drew back his fist and drove it squarely into Kristine's face. For the second time that day, her world went dark.

CHAPTER TWELVE

Inspector Girard stood in the hallway outside the Akbar apartment, listening intently. No sound came from beyond the door. He could hear children laughing in an apartment down the hall. The smell of garlic and meat being cooked infused the corridor, making his mouth water. It had been a long time since breakfast, and here it was already past 8:00 in the evening. He hoped his wife would heat up something good when he finally got home, but who knew when that might be.

He knocked at the door, and after a few moments a middle-aged woman opened it. She was attractive, with smooth olive colored skin and dark brown eyes set beneath long black eyelashes. She wore a floral gown with a matching scarf wrapped around her head.

"Madame Akbar?" he asked. She nodded.

"My name is Inspector Girard, and I am with the Paris police." He showed her his identification card and badge.

"Please, come in," she said, stepping aside so he could enter.

Inspector Girard stepped into the room and looked around, slipping his ID back into his pocket. It was a nice living room, with a red velvet couch along one wall, a gold and purple lap throw draped across the back. Two matching red velvet armchairs sat across from the couch, and an Oriental carpet in reds, black and white was on the floor.

"Several people called the police because they heard a window break in your apartment, then a woman screaming in English," he said. "This woman even climbed from one of your balconies to the next. Can you tell me about that?"

The woman shook her head and waved her hand frivolously. "It was nothing," she began. "My niece was having problems with her boyfriend and wanted to break up with him. He came here, they got into a fight, and he broke the window. My niece was frightened. She went out onto the balcony and screamed for help, and he left." She met Inspector Girard's steady gaze. "It was nothing."

Inspector Girard regarded her face for a moment. "She screamed in English?" he asked, raising his eyebrows inquisitively.

Madame Akbar hesitated, almost imperceptibly, and said, "Yes. She lives in London, and is just visiting us for a few weeks." She smiled confidently.

"And you did not call the police when this happened?"

"No." Madame Akbar paused for a moment. "We are a very private family."

Nodding, Inspector Girard eyed her with suspicion. "May I see the room, please?"

"Of course." Madame Akbar led him into the bedroom where Kristine had been held. A large piece of plywood had been nailed over the broken window. Inspector Girard meandered around the room, looking behind the curtains, beneath the bed. He noticed a pair of hot pink women's tennis shoes. He picked one up and looked inside; size 9½ American; size 41 European. He glanced at Madame Akbar's feet; they were much smaller than that. He set the shoe down again.

"Thank you, *madame*, there will be nothing else." He made his way through the apartment to the front door. "*Au revoir, madame.*"

"*Au revoir, monsieur*," she said, closing the door behind him.

*

Inspector Girard called Agent Hart as soon as he returned to the police station. He told him about the phone calls to the police reporting a woman screaming and climbing over the balcony. "I believe it was Madame Quintana," he said.

"It's a shame that my surveillance team wasn't in place at the apartment. If it had been just 30 minutes later, my men could have rescued her."

"We should ask Madame McKenna if she remembers the shoes that her friend was wearing this morning. A pair of women's pink sport shoes was in the apartment, and they were much too large for Madame Akbar. I am certain they were Madame Quintana's."

"I'll ask her, thanks," said Agent Hart. He sat with his elbows resting on his paper-cluttered desk. He cleared a space, leaned back in his chair, and put his feet up on his desk, the phone wedged between his shoulder and his ear. "Ms. McKenna said Akbar gave her until Saturday morning to get the money. That's not much time."

"I agree. I will have my men talk to our informants in the Arab community to see if anyone has heard anything."

Agent Hart called Claire as soon as he hung up with Inspector Girard. "I just wanted to give you an update. This afternoon the Paris police had multiple reports of a woman screaming from a balcony in the Latin Quarter. Inspector Girard investigated, and found that it was Samir's apartment." He paused for a moment, and asked, "Did you happen to notice what shoes Ms. Quintana was wearing this morning?"

Claire thought for a second. "Hot pink sneakers."

"Inspector Girard found shoes like that in the apartment. We believe that the screaming woman was Ms. Quintana."

Claire felt her pulse quicken with concern. "Any idea where she is now?"

"Not at this time, but we're working on it. I'll keep you posted."

CHAPTER THIRTEEN

When Kristine opened her eyes, she was once again tied to a chair. No more comfortable bedrooms for her; she seemed to be in a cool, musty old cellar. Cobwebs stretched from one wooden floor joist to the next. The room was small, no more than twelve feet by twelve feet. It felt almost like a cave with a damp stone ceiling and a hard dirt floor, and no windows. A set of wooden stairs was against the wall right in front of her, leading to a floor above. A small wooden door was in the wall beneath the staircase. It was no more than four feet high and was made of scarred, worm-holed oaken planks with large corroded metal hinges holding it in place. A rusty iron ring hung just below a small keyhole holding a silver skeleton key. Floor to ceiling shelves lined the other walls, and Kristine could see that they were filled with stacked shoeboxes. Hakim sat on a folding chair across the room from her, watching her with a cold, steady stare. At a safe distance, she figured. Crazy American women, she thought, you don't know what they'll do next. She smiled to herself.

Samir entered the room, his left arm bandaged and in a sling. He walked over and stood right in front of Kristine, glaring down at her with unveiled hostility. "You should not have done that," he seethed with barely controlled contempt. "If your friend does not get the money, it will be my pleasure to behead you."

"So, how much are you asking for?"

Samir didn't speak for a moment, then said, "Ten million American dollars."

Despite the situation, Kristine burst out laughing. "Ten million? Are you nuts? Why not a billion? No, wait, ten billion! Why not ask for ten billion dollars! You'd have as much chance of getting it as you do getting ten *million* dollars." She grew somber, and glared at Samir. "The United States won't negotiate with terrorists, and they're not going to pay any ransom." A heavy silence fell on the room. Kristine looked away, tears welling in her eyes. "I sure as hell wish they would," she said, and after a moment, quietly murmured, "But they won't."

Samir stood for several minutes, just looking at Kristine. "We will see." He turned and left.

Kristine swallowed hard. She met Hakim's eyes, mistrust and suspicion sparking between them like an electric charge. God, Kristine thought, I hope Claire hurries up.

*

Claire tossed and turned all night, and finally gave up on sleep a little after 6 AM. She put on a pot of coffee, and when it was ready took her steaming mug out to the balcony and sat.

The first pink blush of dawn was kissing the eastern sky. It was almost too cool to sit outside in her nightie, but still she sat, cradling the hot mug in both hands, staring blankly at the building across the street. Where was Kristine? What was she doing right now? Sleeping? Being tortured? Claire shook her head in resignation. Nothing I can do about it now. I sure hope Agent Hart and Inspector Girard come through for us and can find her.

*

She decided to go for a run to try and clear her head. She rinsed out her coffee cup, and threw on her sweats. She grabbed her keys and her phone and headed out. She had just entered the Jardin du Luxembourg when her cell phone rang. She stopped running and pulled her phone out of her pocket. Was it Samir again? Apprehensive and panting, she said, "Hello?"

"Claire, this is Agent Hart."

Claire glanced at her watch. It wasn't even 7:00 in the morning. "Did you find her?"

"No, not yet. But we came up with a way to hopefully discover where she is being held. We'll need your help, though. How soon would you be able to get to the Embassy?"

Claire stood with Agent Hart and Inspector Girard in a small room in the Embassy. It was filled with electronics, and dimly lit by a wall of video screens displaying feed from a dozen security cameras surrounding the embassy. A technician sat in front of a large computer screen.

"As I told you, we know where Samir lives, and we know that Ms. Quintana had been held there. We've come up with a way that we might be able to identify where they took her."

"How?"

"We'd like you to call Samir, and ask to talk to Ms. Quintana again. Tell him you might have found a way to get the money, but you want to be certain that she is still alive and ok. Once he gives her the phone, we hope to be able to track her position by the GPS on his cell phone."

Inspector Girard said, "We will then have a rescue team respond…"

"A SWAT team," Agent Hart interrupted.

Inspector Girard gave Agent Hart a steady stare. "Yes, a 'SWAT' team. They will enter the location and hopefully will find Ms. Quintana and free her."

"How soon can we do this?" Claire asked.

"Right now." Agent Hart turned to the electronic technician. "Are you ready?"

"Yes, sir," the man said.

"Go ahead, Claire."

Claire pulled her cell phone out of her purse and dialed Samir's number. He answered on the second ring.

"Samir, it's Claire."

"Do you have the money?"

Claire looked at Agent Hart, who made a circular "keep it going" motion with his finger in the air.

"Not yet, but the State Department is reconsidering and may be able to get you the money by Saturday," she lied. "But before they go any further, they want me to reconfirm that Kristine is still alive. I want to talk to her again."

"You are trying my patience."

Claire's anger rose. "Frankly, I don't give a shit about your patience," she said, even though she knew she should try to remain calm. "I just care about my friend, and I need to know she's ok."

Samir was silent. Claire could hear movement, and it sounded like someone going down wooden steps. "Speak," he eventually said.

"Hello?" Kristine sounded hesitant, but alive.

"Kristine, it's Claire. Are you ok?"

Kristine gave a bitter laugh. "Just peachy."

"See," Samir said, having taken the phone back. "Still alive. For the moment. Do not toy with me, Ms. McKenna," he said angrily, "I am in no mood and will not hesitate to kill your friend."

The technician at the electronic keyboard flashed a "thumbs up" sign. Agent Hart smiled and nodded.

"I won't," said Claire. "I'll be in touch as soon as I hear from the State Department." Claire hung up her phone.

"You are a very good liar," said Inspector Girard, smiling.

"I'm an attorney," said Claire. "Sometimes I lie for a living."

The technician scribbled something on a piece of paper and handed it to Agent Hart. "She's still in the Latin Quarter," he said. "Here's the address."

Agent Hart glanced at the address and handed the paper to Inspector Girard. "Ball's in your court, Inspector."

*

It took less than one hour for the Paris police SWAT team to be deployed. Inspector Girard and Agent Hart sat in a car parked across the street from a shoe store on Rue de Pontoise. Inspector Girard had a pair of binoculars trained on the store. Hiding next to the car were five men of the SWAT team, out of sight of the shoe store. All of the men were dressed in camouflage and wore military helmets and bulletproof vests. They held their automatic rifles at the ready across their chests.

"There is one customer in the store," Inspector Girard said, looking through the binoculars. "But I do not see the clerk." He turned to the leader of the SWAT team. "At your ready, lieutenant."

The lieutenant turned to his men and nodded. The team stood and, heads down and half crouching at the waist, darted across the street, guns at the ready, and entered the store.

Shoes were displayed on glass shelves all along the right and left walls, and a counter with a cash register was at the back of the store. Next to the counter was a cloth curtain that hung over a doorway leading to the stock room. The lone customer was an elderly woman. She was barefooted and sat on a bench with her purse and shoes on the floor, waiting for the clerk to return. When she heard someone come into the shop, she glanced toward the door. Her eyes got huge with fear at the sight of five armed, uniformed men approaching her. The lieutenant put one finger to his lips in a "hush" signal and motioned toward the door, his other hand clutching his automatic rifle. The woman scooped up her purse and shoes and ran out.

The SWAT team cautiously crept toward the back of the store, but before they got there a bearded man in a long cream colored robe came through the curtain carrying two shoeboxes. He froze when he saw the armed men, then surprise filled his face. "Samir!" he shouted. "*Les policiers sont ici!*" One of the SWAT officers ran toward the man and hit him square in the face with the butt of his rifle. The man dropped to the floor, unconscious, blood gushing from his nose. The team ran past him.

Samir shot a glance up the staircase when he heard the man shout, then ran to Kristine's side and pulled a long curved knife out of his robe. "*Hakim, la porte!*" he shouted as he cut the ropes binding Kristine's hands to the chair. He put the knife to her throat and grabbed her arm with his arm that was in the sling. "Get up. If you try to get away, I will kill you."

Hakim ran to the small wooden door, unlocked it, and threw it open. He turned toward Samir, and when he saw that he and Kristine were right behind him, he ran through the door and into the darkness. Hakim pulled out his cell phone and turned on its flashlight. They were in a long, dark, musty tunnel. It looked like it had been bored into gray rock, the uneven stone floor littered with trash. Kristine noticed movement near a pile of garbage, and a rat popped his head out of a paper bag, its eyes glowing red in the light. Kristine screamed, and the rat turned and scurried away into the darkness.

Hakim ran down the tunnel, shining his light in front of him, illuminating the floor a few yards ahead of his feet.

"Move!" shouted Samir, prodding Kristine down the tunnel with his knife, following close behind Hakim and his small circle of light.

Kristine stumbled along in her stocking feet, afraid that she might step on a broken bottle or into something disgusting, but on she went, Samir's knife pressed against her back. Her hands were free, and Samir's arm was still in the sling...should she push him and try to get away? Too risky, she thought. She had no idea where she was, and she didn't think she could find her way in the dark back to the basement where the police were. Plus, she knew she wouldn't be able to run very fast in her stocking feet, and Samir would probably catch her and kill her.

The SWAT team rushed down the stairs and glanced around the basement. The lieutenant noticed the small open door beneath the stairs and went over to it. He took a small pen light out of his pocket and shined it into the shadowy depths. He turned to his team and put one finger to his lips for silence, then motioned for the men to follow him. The men pulled out their own small flashlights, and cautiously advanced into the darkness.

The SWAT team crept along the inky tunnel. It smelled like an old outhouse, the scent of urine and feces almost overpowering. They pressed on, the beam of their lights barely penetrating the darkness. Debris was strewn across the floor, and rats scurried away as the lights approached. After about thirty feet the tunnel split into two paths. The lieutenant motioned for two of the men to follow the left branch, while the lieutenant and the others went to the right. After a short distance the tunnel again split, this time into three paths, all of them consumed in a black void. The lieutenant raised his hand to stop his men and they stood, straining in the silence, willing themselves to hear something, anything. The musty air was as dark and silent as a tomb. The lieutenant shook his head, turned, and the men retraced their steps back to the basement. When they arrived, the other team was already there and waiting for them.

Inspector Girard and Agent Hart sat in the car outside the shoe store. The SWAT team approached their car, and the lieutenant reported in French to Inspector Girard what had happened. When he was finished, Inspector Girard glumly nodded, and the team turned and left.

"They got away."

"How? What happened?" Agent Hart thought for the hundredth time that he really did need to learn French. He hated having Inspector Girard translate everything for him.

"It is not well known, but there are close to two hundred miles of tunnels beneath the city. Some are old mines from hundreds of years ago. In fact, the stones that were used to build Notre Dame came from these mines.

Other tunnels are cemeteries that contain tens of thousands of skulls and bones from the 1700s. Many of these tunnels can still be entered by way of old buildings, and there are tours that will take people through them. It is like a huge maze. Some homeless people even live in the tunnels. When my team entered the basement where Madame Quintana was being held they saw a small door that led into the tunnels. They tried to follow them, but as the tunnels branched, they could not tell which way they had gone. They lost them. We have no idea where they went."

Agent Hart was fuming. If Girard had let him use Navy SEALS for the rescue instead of his own SWAT team, he was certain it would have been a successful rescue, Kristine would be safe, and they would have caught the bad guys. Now, who knows? Will Samir just cut his losses, kill her, and be done with it? How was he going to tell Claire they failed?

CHAPTER FOURTEEN

Kristine had no idea where she was. They had forced her through dark, damp, branching tunnels, twisting and turning, for what seemed like forever. Finally they had reached a small room-like cavern, and Samir lit a tiny candle stuck into the wall. They tied her arms behind her back, and threw her down onto the dirt floor. She rolled over and sat, her back against the wall.

"I have had just about enough of you," Samir said, seething. "Hakim, watch her closely." He left the cave.

Hakim sat on the floor across from her, glaring at Kristine in the candlelight. I'm really screwed, she thought. I'm dead. There's nothing Claire can do now. I just wish I could tell her how much I love her.

*

Claire and Peter were in the Embassy conference room, waiting and hoping in silence that the rescue had been a success and any minute now Agent Hart would walk in with Kristine. But the door opened and Agent Hart came in alone. As soon as they saw his face, Claire's heart sank.

The agent pulled out a chair and sat down heavily. "They got away." He shook his head in disgust.

Claire stared at him in disbelief. "How? How could that happen?"

"Apparently, Paris is honeycombed with miles of tunnels under the city, and they escaped through them."

They sat in silence for several minutes. Finally, Claire said, "What's next? What's the plan now? Kristine is running out of time."

"We'll think of something," Agent Hart said without too much conviction.

Claire clenched her teeth in frustration and anger. Breathing hard and trying to contain her fury, she said, "Not good enough." She stood and walked to the door. "If Kristine's going to get out of this alive, it looks like it'll be up to me." She stormed out of the room.

"Now what?" asked Peter.

Agent Hart shrugged, and shook his head again.

*

Claire took the subway back toward the Latin Quarter, her thoughts muddled, not sure what to do, where to go. She felt like she needed to talk to somebody, somebody to bounce ideas off, and Peter was out of the question. He hadn't been a lot of help lately, and she was sure that he'd feel compelled to go straight to Agent Hart and report anything she said. Who else was there? She walked back toward her apartment, trying to sort everything out, when she thought of Sonja. She headed for American Pie.

The two women sat in Sonja's kitchen. It was like an American kitchen from the 1950's with pale blue walls, a gray formica table with chrome legs, and blue and white gingham curtains pulled back from the window. The refrigerator was the size of an American fridge, much larger than most European ones. The granite countertop held a red

Kitchen Aid Mixer and a toaster, and a coffee maker sat next to a ceramic cookie jar shaped like a teddy bear. It was just after lunch, and street sounds came up to them through the open window. Each of the women had a cup of coffee and a slice of lemon meringue pie on the table in front of them, but neither had done more than just pick at the pie.

"So what do you think?" Claire asked. She cut the tip of the pie off, but then set her fork down, leaving the piece on the plate. She searched Sonja's eyes, hoping for an honest answer.

Sonja slowly shook her head. "I don't know. This Samir seems like a more reasonable guy than the others you've run into. But you can't really take the chance with Kristine's life, can you? And ten million dollars? Geesh!" She shook her head again. "It really sucks that Peter can't help you."

"I know. Part of me understands…if we negotiate with terrorists, where will it end? But on the other hand, hey, this is Kristine! This isn't some theoretical concept…it's the woman I love!"

They sat in silence for several minutes, their coffee growing cold.

After a while, Sonja said, "I wonder if Roshni could help?"

"Really?"

"Well, I know she attends services at the mosque every Friday. That's tomorrow. Maybe there's some gossip floating around, something about a pain in the ass American causing problems." Sonja grinned. "That would be you, my dear."

Claire smiled, despite herself. "That's not the first time someone's called me that. But maybe it would be better if she and I met by ourselves, just one on one. Would you mind calling her to see if we can meet?"

Sonja nodded. "I'll see if she's free this afternoon."

*

Claire was sitting at a quiet table in the back corner of Chez Henri. Most of the lunch crowd had already left, and there were just a handful of people in the restaurant having dessert or coffee. A small cup of coffee was on the table in front of Claire, getting cold. Claire saw Roshni come into the restaurant and look around. When she spotted Claire, she nodded in acknowledgement and made her way to her table.

"Hello, Claire," Roshni said as she approached. Claire stood, and Roshni gave her a *bisou* on each cheek, the "air kisses" that the French often greet their friends with. "Sonja said you wanted to talk to me, but she didn't say why. What's up?"

They both sat down. Claire motioned for a waiter, who approached their table.

"*Oui, madame?*"

"What would you like?" Claire asked Roshni.

"*Une tasse thé avec lait, s'il vous plaît.*"

The waiter nodded and left.

Roshni peered into Claire's face with curiosity.

"First of all, I appreciate you meeting me on such short notice, because it's important."

The waiter returned and placed a cup of tea and a small pitcher of milk in front of Roshni.

"*Merci*," she said as he walked away. She poured a little milk into her cup and slowly stirred the tea.

Claire took a sip of her cold coffee, buying time while she thought about how to approach the problem. "A lot has happened since I met all of you last week." She told Roshni about what happened at Sacré Coeur and the cemetery, Kristine's arrival, and finding the data chip. She told her about Samir, Agent Hart, the botched chip exchanges, and Kristine's abduction.

"And now, after all that, the CIA says they won't help Kristine because the U.S. doesn't negotiate with terrorists."

They sat silently for a few minutes, Roshni staring into her teacup, thinking. Finally, she took a sip of tea, set the cup down, and said, "That's terrible. I'm so sorry. I hope you know that not all Muslims are like that."

"I know, and I don't have anything against Islam. But Sonja thought maybe you could help, Roshni. Maybe you've heard something at the mosque, something that might give us an idea of where Samir is holding Kristine."

Roshni stared again into her teacup. Finally she met Claire's gaze and said, "I'm really sorry, but I can't help you."

"But why not?" Claire asked with more force and frustration than she had intended.

"It's complicated." Roshni glanced toward the people walking by the restaurant on the street, lost in thought.

"How complicated could it be? We're talking about someone murdering my friend!"

The strained silence was almost unbearable. Claire stared intently at Roshni, but she kept her eyes downcast, fixed on her tea, absently stirring the beverage.

Finally, Roshni looked up. "Can you keep a secret?"

Claire was really confused. "I'm an attorney. I'm very good at keeping secrets."

"What I am about to say doesn't go any further than you. Is that understood?" Roshni's eyes searched Claire's.

"All right."

Roshni fiddled again with her teacup, and said, "There are actually two reasons why I can't help you. The first is, if I help you and Samir and the others find out, they'll most certainly kill me. And it is very hard to keep a secret in our mosque. Someone will eventually figure out that I was involved."

Claire nodded. She could feel her hopes for finding Kristine alive begin to evaporate.

"The second reason is more difficult, in many ways. The truth is…" she paused for a moment, considering, then went on, "the truth is that when my husband and I emigrated to the United States, our visas were forged. As a result, my citizenship was based on a lie, and if the United States government ever found out, I'd never be able to return to the States. I'd never be able to see my son again, unless he came here, and he doesn't have that kind of money. And if I help you… if I went to the State Department, I'm afraid they'll discover that I'm not actually a citizen. Better for me to just keep my head down, not say anything, and not draw attention to myself. What is that old saying? 'It's the nail that sticks up that gets hammered down.'"

They sat in silence for a moment. "They're going to kill her," Claire softly said. She looked deeply into Roshni's eyes, pleading.

Roshni was silent for a few minutes, clearly struggling with herself. She sipped her tea, then put the cup down. "OK, here's what I can do. When I'm at the mosque tomorrow, I'll make some indirect inquiries, and see if anyone has heard anything. That's the best I can do."

Claire heaved a sigh of relief. "Thank you." She smiled.

"The service is at noon, so we can meet back here at 2:00. But please, you cannot tell a soul that I am involved."

"Sonja already knows."

"All right, you may tell Sonja, but make sure that she knows that it goes no further. Peter absolutely cannot find out. If he knew, he'd feel obligated to turn me in."

"I understand." Claire took Roshni's hand and gently squeezed it. "Thank you. Thank you very much."

*

Claire headed home. She desperately hoped that Roshni would learn something helpful, but she wasn't too optimistic. It wasn't like anyone at the mosque was likely to come out and say, "Guess what we did yesterday? We kidnapped an American!"

When she got back to the apartment she changed into her sweats and went for a quick run to try and clear her head. As she passed the other people in the park, it struck her how insular people's lives were. Here these people were having a great time and enjoying themselves, while she was in absolute torment worrying about Kristine. They had no idea what was going on with the strangers around them, and probably couldn't have cared less. Not their problem.

She went back home and showered, then grabbed a quick bite for dinner. No matter how hard she tried, she couldn't get the image of Kristine being held in captivity out of her mind. Claire was a person who always had to be in control of a situation, and now she felt utterly helpless. Someone else was calling the shots, and there wasn't a damned thing she could do about it. She shook her head in frustration. There was no way she was going to get ten million dollars for the ransom. Would they really kill her? In her gut, she knew they probably would. She paced across her living room so many times, she was surprised she didn't wear a rut in the carpet.

She glanced at her watch. It seemed like it was hours ago that she ate dinner, but it had only been twenty minutes. It was like the world had stopped revolving, and time had stood still. She finally decided she couldn't stand it anymore, and the best thing would be to just go to bed and hope tomorrow came quickly.

*

It was probably the longest night of Claire's life. She tossed and turned, unable to shut her mind off, unable to shake horrible images of Kristine, maybe being beaten, maybe being raped... Hopefully, Samir would treat her well. He seemed like an honorable man, even if he was a terrorist. An "honorable terrorist". Quite an oxymoron.

By 6:00 AM, she hadn't slept at all, and decided to just get up. She showered and puttered around the apartment, vainly trying to distract herself and force the time to pass. Mid-morning, her phone rang. Was it Agent Hart? Had they come up with a plan? She answered her phone.

"Hello, Ms. McKenna," Samir began. "There has been a change in plans."

Claire suddenly felt sick in the pit of her stomach. Her legs felt like they were going to crumple beneath her, and she barely made it to the couch before she collapsed.

"Is Kristine okay?"

Samir was silent for a moment before responding, "She's fine. I have thought about our demands, and you are correct; the U.S. will not pay ransom for hostages."

"So you'll let her go?" Claire asked excitedly.

She heard Samir snort. "No. While the U.S. will not pay ransom for hostages, in the past they have done prisoner exchanges. They recently traded that soldier Bergdahl for five Taliban prisoners who were being held at Guantanamo Bay, and they have done other prisoner exchanges over the years. So instead of ten million dollars, we are demanding the release of one of our brothers from Guantanamo. His name is Hassan Abdul Khouri."

Claire felt a tiny glimmer of hope in her heart. Would the U.S. agree to this? She knew Samir was right; the government had exchanged hostages in the past, so the precedent was there. Would they do this for Kristine?

"I'll need to talk to the people at the Embassy about that."

"Do not take too long. You have until noon tomorrow."

"That's not enough time!" she exclaimed. "We'll need more time than that. Today's Friday, and the government isn't going to make a big decision like this over a weekend. Give us until Tuesday, at least."

Samir was silent for a moment and said, "Tomorrow," and he was gone.

She called Agent Hart as soon as she hung up. "Samir just called," she began, telling him what had happened. "Do you think we can arrange a prisoner exchange by tomorrow?"

Agent Hart said, "That's not something I'm authorized to decide. I'm going to have to talk to my superiors, and I'll call you back."

Claire nervously paced back and forth in the apartment, her fingers locked behind her neck. "Data," she thought. "I need data to argue my case."

She pulled out her laptop and did a search for "American prisoner exchanges". She was surprised to find that even as far back as the Revolutionary War, the U.S. had taken part in prisoner exchanges. In the 1960s, Gary Powers had been flying his CIA spy plane over Moscow when he was shot down. He was convicted of espionage and spent two years in a Soviet prison before he was exchanged for a Soviet spy being held by the U.S. The more Claire read, the more excited and hopeful she became. The precedents for a prisoner exchange were clearly there. As a lawyer, she knew she could make a case to get Kristine freed in exchange for Khouri.

CHAPTER FIFTEEN

Samir and his wife walked into the cave where Kristine was being held. His wife wore another beautiful full-length gown, emerald green with a floral pattern, with a matching scarf. She carried two bowls of food with spoons sticking out. She gave one to Hakim, and he immediately wolfed down the food. She placed the other on the floor next to Kristine. Samir pulled out a knife and cut Kristine's bonds, his arm still in the sling.

"Eat," he said. His wife crouched on the floor against the wall, watching Kristine.

Kristine looked at the food in her bowl. It looked like a combination of some kind of meat and eggplant. She took a taste. Despite everything else, she had to admit that Samir's wife was one heck of a cook. She caught the wife's eye.

"What's your name?"

The woman stared blankly at Kristine.

"*Comment vous appelez-vous?*" she asked.

The woman said, "Fatima."

"Do not talk!" Samir shouted, glaring at his wife. She withered under his stare, eyes cast downward, intermittently flicking her glance back up at Kristine.

Kristine looked at Samir, and returned her attention to Fatima. She smiled, pointed at the food, nodded and rubbed her belly. Fatima smiled.

173

Samir growled something in Arabic at his wife, and she got up and left. She meekly smiled over her shoulder at Kristine, and nodded.

Kristine quickly ate. When she finished she handed the bowl back to Samir. He said something to Hakim, who came over to Kristine and tied her hands back together. When he was finished, Samir left without saying another word.

*

Agent Hart called Claire a little before noon. "I talked to my superiors," he began. "I'm sorry, but it's not going to be possible to do a prisoner swap."

"But why?" Claire cried out with outrage. "The U.S. has done it dozens of times before! We just did it with that soldier, Bergdahl, for those Taliban terrorists!"

"There are two reasons why we can't do it. First, the exchanges in the past have involved soldiers or CIA personnel, not civilians. We have never negotiated for the release of a civilian."

Claire silently seethed for several minutes. "So an American civilian's life isn't worth saving, is that what you're saying?"

Agent Hart ignored her question, and went on. "The second reason is that the man they want released, Hassan Abdul Khouri, was one of the masterminds behind the bombing of the Golden Gate Bridge in 2014. He's too important of a terrorist for us to release." He was silent for a moment before continuing. "I'm terribly sorry. But rest assured, we will keep trying to find where Kristine is being held and hope to launch another rescue attempt."

"The deadline is noon tomorrow," she said bitterly. "Thanks for nothing."

She hung up, and threw her phone across the room. It bounced off the couch and onto the floor. Her eyes filled with tears of frustration and rage, her teeth clenched. Damn it! Damn it! There had to be a way to get Kristine. There just had to be!

*

Claire was back at Chez Henri a little before 2:00. Roshni was already sitting at a table in the back of the restaurant.

"Did you find out anything?" Claire asked as she sat down.

"There have been some rumors about an American woman being held captive by Samir. I couldn't find out where she is, but it sounds like she's still ok. For now."

"Well, Samir has changed their demands. Instead of money, they now want the release of a prisoner from Gitmo. I talked to the CIA agent I've been dealing with, and he said they won't do it." She leaned back in her chair, and shook her head. "I don't know what to do. I'm afraid they'll kill her."

"Have you said anything about this to anyone? Does Samir know that there won't be an exchange?"

Claire shook her head.

"I may have an idea. Where are you staying?"

"In an apartment on Rue Cujas."

Roshni looked at her watch, then took a piece of paper and pen from her purse and slid them across the table to Claire. "Please write down your address." Claire did as she was told. As Roshni put the paper in her purse, she said,

175

"I'll meet you in front of your apartment at 4:00 this afternoon. Do not tell anyone about this, do you understand?"

*

Claire was on the street in front of her apartment a few minutes before 4:00. She gazed up and down the street. Only a few pedestrians were out. It was too early for people to go out for their Friday evening socialization. A black Mercedes slowly drove down the street. As it approached, Claire could see a person in a black burqa behind the wheel. Her pulse quickened when it stopped in front of her and the passenger side window rolled down. She was on the verge of running away when she heard Roshni's voice say, "Get in."

She climbed into the car. "What the heck?" she asked. "Why the burqa?"

"I don't want to be recognized if someone sees me. This is a rented car, too, just in case someone would recognize my Volvo." She pulled out into the street and drove. "I admit maybe I'm being a little paranoid, but I just don't want to take any chances. I'd rather be safe than very, very sorry. Or dead."

They drove south from the Latin Quarter into the 13th arrondissement, past a large roundabout at the Place d'Italie, and parked down the street from an apartment building on Rue Coypel.

"Where are we?" Claire asked.

"You see that apartment building, number 38?" Roshni pointed down the street. "Samir lives in that building. I know you said they've moved Kristine, but I

176

thought that maybe we could watch and if he comes out, we could follow him. Maybe he'll lead us to Kristine."

"Worth a shot," Claire said.

They sat in the car in silence for a long time, focused on the apartment. No one entered or left.

After nearly an hour, Claire turned to her friend and asked, "Do you want some coffee or something? I think I saw a *patisserie* down the street, and I bet they have coffee."

Roshni pointed through the windshield. "Look, someone's coming out."

As they watched, a small boy, maybe 4 years old, came out onto the sidewalk. He was dressed in a long white robe and promptly knelt on the sidewalk, pulled out some sidewalk chalk, and began to draw.

"That's Samir's son, Jabar," Roshni said. "So someone is home. Maybe Samir, or maybe his wife, Fatima."

They watched the little boy for a few long minutes as he drew on the sidewalk. Neither woman spoke. Then Claire suddenly said, "Start the car. I'll be right back." Claire opened her door and stepped out onto the street.

"What are you doing?" shouted Roshni after her. She started the engine.

Claire walked up to the little boy. He was intent on his artwork and didn't even look up as she approached. Claire glanced up and down the street; no one was in sight. Claire bent over, put her arm under the boy's belly, and scooped him up, his limbs dangling helplessly. He started screaming, and Claire ran back to the car, his arms and legs thrashing. She threw the little boy in the back seat and climbed in after him.

"Drive! Drive!"

Roshni turned in her seat and looked back at her. Claire was certain that if she could have seen Roshni's face beneath the burqa, it would have been horrified.

"What are you doing?" Roshni yelled.

"Just drive, damn it!"

Roshni stepped on the accelerator, and they tore away from the curb and down the street. Claire could see the boy's chalk still on the sidewalk where he had dropped it.

"Claire, this is crazy! This is kidnapping! Kidnappers get twenty years in prison in France!"

"There's an old American saying: 'Turnabout is fair play'. Samir has someone I love, and now I have someone he loves. We'll swap, and that will be that."

Roshni said something to the boy in French, and he settled down in his seat and stopped screaming. He sniffed once or twice, and wiped his tears on his sleeve. He looked at Claire with his big brown eyes. She smiled at him and patted him on his knee.

"It's going to be ok," she said, and smiled. He just looked at her with fear.

"I don't think he speaks any English," Roshni said.

"Do you think he'll know who you are?" Claire asked.

"I don't think so. We've never spoken before, and since I'm wearing the burqa, he won't recognize me. Where are we going?"

"Someplace safe. Not my apartment, because they know where I live and that would be the first place they'll look."

Roshni heaved a sigh. "All right, we'll go to my house. Jabar will never be able to find it again or tell his father where he was. But if I get caught, if they catch me and kill me, I'll never forgive you."

*

Roshni's apartment was in an upscale neighborhood of Paris, near the arc de triomphe. There was a parking garage beneath the building and she pulled into her designated slot. Claire glanced around, and saw no one else in the garage. They got out of the car and, taking Jabar by the hand, quickly walked to the elevator and took it to the third floor.

The apartment was really quite beautiful. A tall cathedral ceiling soared over a comfortable cream-colored living room filled with soft velvet chairs. A red, green and yellow Oriental carpet was in the center of the room, and a low coffee table sat in front of a vintage divan sofa. Two antique side tables flanked the sofa, each holding a cream colored porcelain table lamp with gilded trim and a pink rose on it, capped by an ornate, cream colored tasseled shade. White lace curtains cascaded over tall windows.

"This is magnificent," said Claire, gazing appreciatively around the room.

"Thanks."

Jabar said something to Roshni in French. She replied in French, and he nodded.

"He's hungry. I'll get him something to eat." Roshni took Jabar by the hand and went into the kitchen.

Claire sat on the couch. She had to admit; she really hadn't thought this through when she snatched Jabar. She tried to think of how to approach this, what to do next. Roshni was right; she was guilty of kidnapping, and Roshni was now an accomplice. But wasn't it only fair? Would the police really prosecute her, given the situation? She was certain that Samir wouldn't press charges, since he had kidnapped someone, himself. And she doubted that Agent Hart would pursue kidnapping charges. But Inspector Girard? She had no idea. A flicker of panic started in her belly…my god, what have I done?

Roshni and Jabar came back into the living room, Jabar munching on a banana.

"Now what?" Roshni asked.

Claire shook her head. "I'm really not sure. Should I call Agent Hart and tell him what's going on? So they can grab Samir when we make the exchange?"

"I wouldn't do that. It's pretty risky. This was a kidnapping, after all, and he could arrest you. And I certainly don't want to be exposed as an accomplice."

"But would Agent Hart do that? After all, he's CIA, not the police, and a kidnapping in Paris probably isn't under his jurisdiction. Inspector Girard would probably arrest us, but Agent Hart?" She shook her head. "Maybe not."

The two women sat in silence for a few minutes. Jabar silently munched on his banana, glancing with curiosity from one woman to the other.

"Better call Samir and set up the exchange," Roshni said.

Claire nodded, then pulled out her cell phone and dialed. She could feel nervous sweat start to bead on her forehead, and her pulse quicken. All the chips were on the table now. Do or die. Literally.

Samir answered on the second ring. "I hope you have arranged the exchange for brother Khouri, Ms. McKenna."

"No, that's not going to happen," said Claire. "But there's a different exchange that I think you might be interested in." She put the phone to Jabar's ear and nodded.

"*Allô?*" he said in a meek little, uncertain voice.

Claire took the phone back and put it to her own ear just in time to hear Samir's panicked voice. "Jabar?"

"That's right, Samir. I have Jabar," she said in a cool, firm voice. "Now I have someone you love, and you have someone I love. It's time we trade."

The line was silent for a moment. Claire could hear Samir's slow, controlled breathing. "If you harm him," he began in a steady voice, "if you hurt one hair on his head, I will hunt you down and kill you, your family, everyone you care about. And your friend here will be the first to die."

"It doesn't have to come to that," Claire calmly said. She suddenly felt the same confidence, the same sense of power that she felt in court when she had her opponent on the ropes. She was in command. She knew it, and she knew that Samir knew it, too. "I have no intention of hurting Jabar, as long as you give me Kristine and she hasn't been hurt. Here's what's going to happen."

CHAPTER SIXTEEN

Hakim looked up as Samir came into the cavern. He angrily threw a pair of hot pink tennis shoes at Kristine.

"Put these on," Samir ordered.

"It's hard to do when I'm like this," Kristine said, holding up her bound hands.

He pulled out a long knife and walked over to where Kristine sat, and sliced her ropes. "Hurry up."

*

Claire, her burqa-clad friend and Jabar sat in the Jardin du Luxembourg at a small table in front of a concession stand. The little boy was facing the counter, his back to the gardens, eating an ice cream cone. She looked at her friend, and even though she couldn't read her face, she knew she would be glad when this was all over. They all would be. To think that this was where it all began just a week ago. Hopefully this is where it would soon end.

Claire glanced around the gardens. A man sat on a bench, calmly reading a newspaper. A woman jogged in place further down the path. They had no idea about the life and drama that was unfolding right in front of them.

She looked at Jabar and he met her eyes. She smiled, and he smiled back. He really was a cute little guy.

Claire gazed past Jabar into the garden and her heart lept. There was Kristine, about fifty yards away, walking straight toward her. Samir walked at her side, one arm around her waist, the other in a sling but gripping her arm. There was a jacket draped over Kristine's hands, undoubtedly hiding her bound wrists. Claire grinned.

Samir stopped and glared at Claire. He released Kristine, and gave her a push. She briefly stumbled, then stood up straight, pausing for a moment. She started walking toward Claire, and after a few steps, broke into a run, the jacket that had been draped over her hands fell to the ground, exposing her hands that were tied together.

When it was certain that Kristine was safely away from Samir, Claire tapped Jabar on his hand. When the boy looked up at her, Claire pointed behind him. "Look."

Jabar turned. "Papa!" he screamed, dropped his ice cream cone and ran toward his father.

Samir scooped the boy up, covering him in kisses, twirling around with him in delight. Jabar buried his face in his father's chest and tightly clung to him.

Claire got up and ran to meet Kristine. She wrapped her arms around her, frantically kissing her on the lips, the cheeks, the forehead. Kristine started to cry.

"Thank God you're ok!" Claire said as she untied Kristine's hands. Once free, Kristine fell into Claire's arms, sobbing.

"Thank you, thank you!" Kristine exclaimed. She sniffled, holding Claire at arm's length, looking into her eyes. "I love you so much," Kristine said. "I'm so sorry for how I treated you."

"No, I'm sorry. It was all my fault," Claire said. "I should have been there more for you."

Kristine smiled and wiped her eyes. "Well, you sure came through in the pinch!"

"I can't believe it's finally over," Claire said, shaking her head. She reached into her pocket and pulled out the small gold ring and slid it back on Kristine's little finger. "Back where it belongs."

She kissed Kristine on the cheek.

Claire looked past Kristine at Samir. The woman in the park who had been jogging in place and the man with the newspaper both ran over to Samir, guns drawn. Samir saw them, set his son down on the ground, and raised his hands high over his head. The man took Jabar by the hand, while the woman pulled Samir's hands one by one behind his back and handcuffed him. The four of them walked toward the park entrance.

Claire furrowed her brows, thoroughly confused.

"I'm glad everything worked out," Agent Hart said as he came from behind the concession stand.

"What are you doing here?" Claire was stunned.

"We were keeping an eye on Samir's apartment, hoping we could follow him to where they were keeping her." He smiled. "Seems like great minds think alike. When we saw you take the boy, we followed you and ended up here."

Claire put her arm around Kristine's waist. She hated to ask, but knew she had to. "Am I in trouble for taking the boy?"

"What boy?" He pretended to be confused for a minute and grinned. "Not my jurisdiction."

He turned to the woman in the burqa. "Who's your friend?"

The woman pulled off the burqa's hood. Sonja grinned at Agent Hart.

"We haven't met," she said. "I'm Sonja."

"You all did well," Agent Hart said. "We got the bad guy, your friend is safe... you should all be proud of yourselves. If you ever want a job with the CIA, just give me a call."

"I think I'll pass," Claire said.

Kristine smiled and gave Claire another hug. "Let's go home."

EPILOGUE

This time, the loud drone of the jet engines didn't bother Claire at all. They sat in first class seats, a glass of white wine on each of their tray tables. The flight attendant came by and topped off their glasses.

"It was nice of the CIA to buy us first class tickets," Kristine said.

"It was the least they could do."

"So Roshni was the one who actually helped you? Not Sonja?"

"Well, they both helped," Claire said, taking a sip of wine. "Roshni helped me grab Jabar, but she was afraid she'd be seen at the Jardin du Luxembourg, and some people in the Arab community might come after her and retaliate. So Sonja stepped up and took her place for the exchange."

"How did Agent Hart know to have agents waiting at the Luxembourg Gardens?"

"Apparently, once they saw me grab Jabar, they tapped my cell phone and heard us set up the exchange. I don't know how legal that was, but oh, well, it worked out for the best."

They sat quietly for a few moments before Kristine said, "You met some really nice people, didn't you?"

Claire nodded. "The best."

"Agent Hart seemed nice enough at my de-briefing. He said they were able to track down Hakim, and he gave up almost a dozen other terrorists. I don't think Hakim had the same fire in his belly for 'the cause' that Samir had." She took a sip of wine, and set her glass down on the tray table. "I wish I could have met Inspector Girard."

"He's a sweet man. It's too bad I didn't get a chance to say goodbye to him. Hart said that when he told him you were free and they had captured Samir, he was very happy. He seemed more humane than Hart, but maybe that's just the difference between the police and the CIA. Or the difference between being French and American. Inspector Girard will be charging Samir with kidnapping, but I think the CIA's terrorism charges will trump that. "

"Did Inspector Girard find out that you had taken Jabar?"

Claire laughed. "Yeah. Samir kept screaming that I had kidnapped his son, but no one seemed to give a damn. I guess that even Inspector Girard figured it was just 'a means to an end', and since we got on the plane before Inspector Girard could officially interview us… oh, well."

"Can we ever go back to Paris, or will there be Wanted Posters up for you? Mass murderer, kidnapper…you must be on the Parisian Most Wanted List!" Kristine laughed.

"Agent Hart said that Inspector Girard told him we'd be welcome to come back any time we want."

Kristine took Claire's hand and gave it a squeeze. "I would like to go back someday, but I don't think I could do it any time soon."

The flight attendant came and stood next to their seats. "Would you ladies like beef or chicken? We have filet mignon in a Roquefort cabernet sauce or chicken cordon bleu with gratin dauphinois potatoes."

Claire smiled contentedly, and leaned back in her seat. "Ah, life is so good!"

About the Author

Joan L. Anderson fell in love with Paris and the French people the first time she visited the city in 1998. Since then, she returns to France whenever possible.

After being together for 25 years, Joan and her partner, Barbara, were finally able to marry in 2014. They live outside Seattle, Washington, with their two dogs.

Other Titles Available From Triplicity Publishing

Wrecked by Sydney Canyon. To most people, the *Duchess* is a myth formed by old pirates tales, but to Reid Cavanaugh, a Caribbean island bum and one of the best divers and treasure hunters in the world, it's a real, seventeenth century pirate ship—the holy grail of underwater treasure hunting. Reid uses the same cunning tactics she always has before setting out to find the lost ship. However, she is forced to bring her business partner's daughter along as collateral this time because he doesn't trust her. Neither woman is thrilled, but being cooped up on a small dive boat for days, forces them to get know each other quickly.

Arson by Austen Thorne. Madison Drake is a detective for the Stetson Beach Police Department. The last thing she wants to do is show a new detective the ropes, especially when a fire investigation becomes arson to cover up a murder. Madison butts heads with Tara, her trainee, deals with sarcasm from Nic, her ex-girlfriend who is a patrol officer, and finds calm in the chaos of police work with Jamie, her best friend who is the county medical examiner. Arson is the first of many in a series of novella episodes surrounding the fictional Stetson Beach Police Department and Detective Madison Drake.

Change of Heart by KA Moll. Courtney Holloman is a woman at the top of her game. She's successful, wealthy, and a highly sought after Washington lobbyist. She has money, her job, booze, and nothing else. In quiet moments, against her will, her mind drifts back to her days in high school and to all that she gave up. Jack Camdon is a complex woman, and yet not at all. She is also a woman who has never moved beyond the sudden and unexplained departure of her high school sweetheart, her lover, and her soul mate. When circumstances bring Courtney back to town two decades later, their paths will cross. Will it be too late?

Mommies (Bridal Series book 3) by Graysen Morgen. Britton and her wife Daphne have been married for a year and a half and are happy with their life, until Britton's mother hounds her to find out why her sister Bridget hasn't decided to have children yet. This prompts Daphne to bring up the big subject of having kids of their own with Britton. Britton hadn't really thought much about having kids, but her love for Daphne makes her see life and their future together in a whole new way when they decide to become mommies.

Haunting Love by K.A. Moll. Anna Crestwood was raised in the strict beliefs of a religious sect nestled in the foothills of the Smoky Mountains. She's a lesbian with a ton of baggage—fearful, guilty, and alone. Very few things would compel her to leave the familiar. The job offer of a lifetime is one of them. Gabe Garst is a police officer. She's also a powerful medium. Her work with juvenile delinquents and ghosts is all that keeps her going. Inside she's dead, certain that her capacity to love is buried six feet under. Anna and Gabe's paths cross. Their attraction is immediate, but they hold back until all hope seems lost.

Rapture & Rogue by Sydney Canyon. Taren Rauley is happy and in a good relationship, until the one person she thought she'd never see again comes back into her life. She struggles to keep the past from colliding with the present as old feelings she thought were dead and gone, begin to haunt her. In college, Gianna Revisi was a mastermind, ring-leading, crime boss. Now, she has a great life and spends her time running Rapture and Rogue, the two establishments she built from the ground up. The last person she ever expects to see walk into one of them, is the girl who walked out on her, breaking her heart five years ago.

Second Chance by Sydney Canyon. After an attack on her convoy, Marine Corps Staff Sergeant, Darien Hollister, must learn to live without her sight. When an experimental procedure allows her to see again, Darien is torn, knowing someone had to die in order for this to happen.
She embarks on a journey to personally thank the donor's family, but is too stunned to tell them the truth. Mixed emotions stir inside of her as she slowly gets to the know the people that feel like so much more than strangers to her. When the truth finally comes out, Darien walks away, taking the second chance that she's been given to go back to the only life she's ever known, but she's not the only one with a second chance at life.

Meant to Be by Graysen Morgen. Brandt is about to walk down the aisle with her girlfriend, when an unexpected chain of events turns her world upside down, causing her to question the last three years of her life. A chance encounter sparks a mix of rage and excitement that she has never felt before. Summer is living life and following her dreams, all the while, harboring a huge secret that could ruin her career. She believes that some things are better kept in the dark, until she has her third run-in with a woman she had hoped to never see again, and gives into temptation. Brandt and Summer start believing everything happens for a reason as they learn the true meaning of meant to be.

Coming Home by Graysen Morgen. After tragedy derails TJ Abernathy's life, she packs up her three year old son and heads back to Pennsylvania to live with her grandmother on the family farm. TJ picks back up where she left off eight years earlier, tending to the fruit and nut tree orchard, while learning her grandmother's secret trade. Soon, TJ's high school sweetheart and the same girl who broke her heart, comes back into her life, threatening to steal it away once again. As the weeks turn into months and tragedy strikes again, TJ realizes coming home was the best thing she could've ever done.

Special Assignment by Austen Thorne. Secret Service Agent Parker Meeks has her hands full when she gets her new assignment, protecting a Congressman's teenage daughter, who has had threats made on her life and been whisked away to a Christian boarding school under an alias to finish out her senior year. Parker is fine with the assignment, until she finds out she has to go undercover as a Canon Priest. The last thing Parker expects to find is a beautiful, art history teacher, who is intrigued by her in more ways than one.

Miracle at Christmas by Sydney Canyon. A Modern Twist on the Classic Scrooge Story. Dylan is a power-hungry lawyer who pushed away everything good in her life to become the best defense attorney in the, often winning the worst cases and keeping anyone with enough money out of jail. She's visited on Christmas Eve by her deceased law partner, who threatens her with a life in hell like his own, if she doesn't change her path. During the course of the night, she is taken on a journey through her past, present, and future with three very different spirits.

Bella Vita by Sydney Canyon. Brady is the First Officer of the crew on the Bella Vita, a luxury charter yacht in the Caribbean. She enjoys the laidback island lifestyle, and is accustomed to high profile guests, but when a U.S. Senator charters the yacht as a gift to his beautiful twin daughters who have just graduated from college and a few of their friends, she literally has her hands full.

Brides (Bridal Series book 2) by Graysen Morgen. Britton Prescott is dating the love of her life, Daphne Attwood, after a few tumultuous events that happened to unravel at her sister's wedding reception, seven months earlier. She's happy with the way things are, but immense pressure from her family and friends to take the next step, nearly sends her back to the single life. The idea of a long engagement and simple wedding are thrown out the window, as both families take over, rushing Britton and Daphne to the altar in a matter of weeks.

Cypress Lake by Graysen Morgen. The small town of Cypress Lake is rocked when one murder after another happens. Dani Ricketts, the Chief Deputy for the Cypress

Lake Sheriff's Office, realizes the murders are linked. She's surprised when the girl that broke her heart in high school has not only returned home, but she's also Dani's only suspect. Kristen Malone has come back to Cypress Lake to put the past behind her so that she can move on with her life. Seeing Dani Ricketts again throws her off-guard, nearly derailing her plans to finally rid herself and her family of Cypress Lake.

Crashing Waves by Graysen Morgen. After a tragic accident, Pro Surfer, Rory Eden, spends her days hiding in the surf and snowboard manufacturing company that she built from the ground up, while living her life as a shell of the person that she once was. Rory's world is turned upside when a young surfer pursues her, asking for the one thing she can't do. Adler Troy and Dr. Cason Macauley from Graysen Morgen's bestselling novel: *Falling Snow*, make an appearance in this romantic adventure about life, love, and letting go.

Bridesmaid of Honor (Bridal Series book 1) by Graysen Morgen. Britton Prescott's best friend is getting married and she's the maid of honor. As if that isn't enough to deal with, Britton's sister announces she's getting married in the same month and her maid of honor is her best friend Daphne, the same woman who has tormented Britton for years. Britton has to suck it up and play nice, instead of scratching her eyes out, because she and Daphne are in both weddings. Everyone is counting on them to behave like adults.

Falling Snow by Graysen Morgen. Dr. Cason Macauley, a high-speed trauma surgeon from Denver meets

Adler Troy, a professional snowboarder and sparks fly. The last thing Cason wants is a relationship and Adler doesn't realize what's right in front of her until it's gone, but will it be too late?

Fate vs. Destiny by Graysen Morgen. Logan Greer devotes her life to investigating plane crashes for the National Transportation Safety Board. Brooke McCabe is an investigator with the Federal Aviation Association who literally flies by the seat of her pants. When Logan gets tangled in head games with both women will she choose fate or destiny?

Just Me by Graysen Morgen. Wild child Ian Wiley has to grow up and take the reins of the hundred year old family business when tragedy strikes. Cassidy Harland is a little surprised that she came within an inch of picking up a gorgeous stranger in a bar and is shocked to find out that stranger is the new head of her company.

Love Loss Revenge by Graysen Morgen. Rian Casey is an FBI Agent working the biggest case of her career and madly in love with her girlfriend. Her world is turned upside when tragedy strikes. Heartbroken, she tries to rebuild her life. When she discovers the truth behind what really happened that awful night she decides justice isn't good enough, and vows revenge on everyone involved.

Natural Instinct by Graysen Morgen. Chandler Scott is a Marine Biologist who keeps her private life private. Corey Joslen is intrigued by Chandler from the moment she meets her. Chandler is forced to finally open her life up to Corey. It backfires in Corey's face and sends her running. Will either woman learn to trust her natural instinct?

Secluded Heart by Graysen Morgen. Chase Leery is an overworked cardiac surgeon with a group of best friends that have an opinion and a reason for everything. When she meets a new artist named Remy Sheridan at her best friend's art gallery she is captivated by the reclusive woman. When Chase finds out why Remy is so sheltered will she put her career on the line to help her or is it too difficult to love someone with a secluded heart?

In Love, at War by Graysen Morgen. Charley Hayes is in the Army Air Force and stationed at Ford Island in Pearl Harbor. She is the commanding officer of her own female-only service squadron and doing the one thing she loves most, repairing airplanes. Life is good for Charley, until the day she finds herself falling in love while fighting for her life as her country is thrown haphazardly into World War II. Can she survive being in love and at war?

Fast Pitch by Graysen Morgen. Graham Cahill is a senior in college and the catcher and captain of the softball team. Despite being an all-star pitcher, Bailey Michaels is young and arrogant. Graham and Bailey are forced to get to know each other off the field in order to learn to work together on the field. Will the extra time pay off or will it drive a nail through the team?

Submerged by Graysen Morgen. Assistant District Attorney Layne Carmichael had no idea that the sexy woman she took home from a local bar for a one night stand would turn out to be someone she would be prosecuting months later. Scooter is a Naval Officer on a submarine who changes women like she changes uniforms. When she is accused of a heinous crime she is shocked to see her latest conquest sitting across from her as the prosecuting attorney.

Vow of Solitude by Austen Thorne. Detective Jordan Denali is in a fight for her life against the ghosts from her past and a Serial Killer taunting her with his every move. She lives a life of solitude and plans to keep it that way. When Callie Marceau, a curious Medical Examiner, decides she wants in on the biggest case of her career, as well as, Jordan's life, Jordan is powerless to stop her.

Igniting Temptation by Sydney Canyon. Mackenzie Trotter is the Head of Pediatrics at the local hospital. Her life takes a rather unexpected turn when she meets a flirtatious, beautiful fire fighter. Both women soon discover it doesn't take much to ignite temptation.

One Night by Sydney Canyon. While on a business trip, Caylen Jarrett spends an amazing night with a beautiful stripper. Months later, she is shocked and confused when that same woman re-enters her life. The fact that this stranger could destroy her career doesn't bother her. C.J. is more terrified of the feelings this woman stirs in her. Could she have fallen in love in one night and not even known it?

Fine by Sydney Canyon. Collin Anderson hides behind a façade, pretending everything is fine. Her workaholic wife and best friend are both oblivious as she goes on an emotional journey, battling a potentially hereditary disease that her mother has been diagnosed with.

The only person who knows what is really going on, is Collin's doctor. The same doctor, who is an acquaintance that she's always been attracted to, and who has a partner of her own.

Shadow's Eyes by Sydney Canyon. Tyler McCain is the owner of a large ranch that breeds and sells different types of horses. She isn't exactly thrilled when a Hollywood movie producer shows up wanting to film his latest movie on her property. Reegan Delsol is an up and coming actress who has everything going for her when she lands the lead role in a new film, but there one small problem that could blow the entire picture.

Light Reading: A Collection of Novellas by Sydney Canyon. Four of Sydney Canyon's novellas together in one book, including the bestsellers Shadow's Eyes and One Night.

Visit us at www.tri-pub.com